GARLIC QUEEN

A NOVEL BY

WENDY LORD

D1518381

Dedicated to my sisters (my best friends)
Sherrie Grimes
Bonnie Brady
Vanyanna Kendall

You are always available and willing to help me through the sticky parts...
in writing a book and in life.
I love you

FOREWORD

Sometimes when we get to know the people around us or get an unbiased glimpse of our own lives, it's easy to see how one stroke of bad luck, one careless decision can lead to another and that to another until we are smothering under an absolute avalanche of misfortune.

So many people grow up feeling abandoned, rejected and hopeless. One person's decision or action can create a hell for someone else, and one person's kindness and respect can turn it all around again.

Youth speaker and teen expert Josh Shipp says, "Every kid is one caring adult away from being a success story."

That's an echo of this ancient wisdom expressed by J.M. Barrie, "Always be kinder than necessary. Everyone is dealing with something."

CHAPTER ONE

*S*amantha Sullivan eased up on the gas pedal as she approached an even denser bank of fog. At home, driving on the coast of California, there was always plenty of fog to deal with. But this felt different: closer, damper, greener somehow. This was Maine.

She hadn't remembered her childhood home being so far from Logan Airport in Boston. The road up from Portland was familiar because there was only one road, and that was Route 1. But familiar or not, tonight, it felt unusually long and lonely. Samantha shifted in her seat to lean closer to the windshield, hoping that would improve visibility.

"Jesus, please! Keep me awake!" she muttered. "This trip is taking forever."

She turned up the heat underneath the front seat. *Wow! Needing the heat in June? Just like February in North Hills.* When she'd left Maine as a twelve-year-old, Samantha had really missed home, and she was depressed for weeks! But California's weather was one thing she never complained about.

Up ahead, she could see where the shoulder widened

significantly, offering an invitation to pull off the road. She did so, and turned off the engine.

Sam sat in the stillness for a minute and tried to loosen the tension in her neck. She leaned across the seat to peer up out of the passenger side window, and in that instant, Sam knew she had been here before. Here in this exact situation.

"GRAMMY, *The fog looks fluffy. Can I feel it?*"

"*You can try. Roll down the window and stand up on the seat.*"

I stood up,and stretched myself out the window and into the fog. I stared over the guardrail. "It looks like a cloud, wif trees stickin' up."

"*I'll tell you what, Sammi. Look real good at that. When we get home, draw a picture of what it looks like. Then, on a nice sunny day, we'll drive back down here and see how different it is.*"

Headlights pulled up behind our car.

"*I think that's the state police,*" *Grammy said.*

I quickly sat down and put on my seat belt.

"*Good evening, Ma'am. Are you having trouble?*"

"*No, officer, just stopped for a little break.*"

"*I wanted to feel the fog, "I volunteered.*

"*What did it feel like?" asked the officer.*

"*I didn't feel nuffing. Jus' kinda wet," I said.*

"*By the way, miss, those are very sparkly shoes you have on.*"

I looked at my legs and feet stretched out in front of me, just barely touching the glove compartment. "These are my GOOD shoes," I said.

"*I can see why they would be. Have you been someplace special today?*"

I was going to tell him we'd been to see the judge, but Grammy jumped right in and answered, "We always say that any day can be special if you wear your good shoes."

"Yes, ma'am. That makes a lot of sense. Now, ladies, there's a gas station just a few miles further on, and it's a much safer place to stop."

"Thank you, officer," Grammy said. "I know the place. We live in Royalty, so we don't have far to get home. But I would appreciate your driving ahead of us so we can see your tail lights until we can get out of this fog a little further inland."

We waited until the trooper pulled out ahead of us and followed him up the road.

"Grammy, are you mad?"

"No, sweetie, why do you think I'm mad?"

"Your little finger is jumping up and down."

"Oh, sorry, that's just because I'm thinking."

"'Bout what?"

"Grown-up stuff. That's all."

SAMANTHA FIGURED she must have been pretty little at that time because her grandmother was still "Grammy" then. It wasn't until she was older, maybe 5 or 6 years old, that "Grammy" became "Bama." That was the name she and her friend Cherie had come up with to settle the arguments about whose grandmother she actually was. (*Mine!*, thought Sam.)

Only now, Bama was gone. Tall, thin, sweet and kind… but gone.

Tonight Samantha, as the sole heir, had come back to sort out the house and figure out what came next.

Once she left Route 1, the road was more narrow and dark, and wound itself through thick spruce and tall pines and around the occasional new log home or dilapidated barn and split-rail fence.

Finally, her headlights picked up a reflection from the

little pond at the bottom of the driveway. And there was the farmstand with the fading sign that read, ROYALTY GARLIC. Sam knew that in early June, there wouldn't be garlic for sale, probably just lots of spinach. But then again, no, not this June.

She pulled into the driveway and parked in the level space at the top of the hill. She found her way up the steps using her cell phone's flashlight. The lawyer had mailed her Bama's keys, which she fished out of the bottom of her bag to let herself in.

The light switches didn't work, but right then, all she wanted was to lie down and go to sleep. She grabbed the quilt from the back of the sofa, flopped down and was out in a minute.

HOURS LATER, as she regained consciousness, Sam was aware of being enveloped in a familiar cocoon of safety and comfort, a feeling swiftly followed by a sudden sharp pang of grief along with the uneasy air of all the unknowns which lay ahead of her.

Like every morning of her life since she was little, Sam stood and stretched. She gazed out of the picture window, then stretched again. *Push the mountain, Lift the sky...*

"PUSH THE MOUNTAIN, Lift the Sky, Floating angels learn to fly"
    "Stop, Bama. This isn't real chai tea, is it?"
    "No, Sammi, Chai tea is something we drink. This is Tai Chi. Although you're correct. It's not REAL tai chi. I only took classes for about a year, many years ago. Nowadays, I do exercises that

feel good and I make up names and rhymes to help me remember what to do."

"Well, I don't want to say 'angels' anymore."

Bama stopped stretching and looked at me. "Why would that be?"

"Cause angels don't have to learn stuff. They live with God, so they just know how."

"How do you know what angels do?"

"Cherie says they told her that at church."

"Well, they would know, I suppose. So, okay. Think of something else we can say."

"How 'bout 'little birdies learn to fly.'"

"Birdies it is."

———

SAMANTHA PUSHED THE MOUNTAIN, lifted the sky, and floated the little birdies down through the air to her sides again. On the fourth repetition, her eye caught something run across the front yard and scoot under the steps. A cat followed close behind it.

For a few seconds, there was general shrieking and squawking under the porch with fur and feathers flying.

Sam abandoned her morning routine and ventured out onto the porch. The gray tabby shot out again and this time ducked under her rental car, briefly poking his nose out from the wheel well on top of the front passenger-side tire.

A large golden hen came strutting out across the lawn, announcing her victory with every step. Samantha watched the chicken march off to the left, back towards the henhouse, which she could just see peeking out from the trees.

I totally forgot about the chickens! thought Samantha, *I have to pee, and I'm still in the clothes I traveled in. I'd better get myself together and go see what's going on with those silly birds.*

TWENTY MINUTES later as Samantha crossed the lawn she noticed it had been recently mowed. Someone, probably the guy across the street, was still looking after the property.

Approaching the hen house, she was greeted by a most unexpected sight. In the enclosure was a child who wore a New England Patriots jersey tucked into a huge pink tutu. Wispy-fine light brown hair strayed out from under a John Deere baseball cap. The skinniest legs on the planet ended in pink rubber boots with pig faces on the toes. The door to the pen was standing open, chickens were milling about, poking at the boots while the child filled the water container.

"I don't know who you are," said Samantha. "But I'm pretty sure you're not Tom Brady."

The little girl straightened up and turned around.

"She's dead," she said.

"Who is?" asked Samantha, thinking of the cat or the feisty hen.

"Bama. Bama's dead."

"Yes, I know, honey. I'm her granddaughter from California. I'm here to figure out what's next."

"Well," said the perhaps-seven-year-old. "What's next is breakfast. Mom said to bring you."

"Who's your mom?" said Sam.

"Cherie Pelletier"

"You're Cherie's daughter?"

"Yeah, duh. She's my mom, so I'm her daughter. That's how it works. Are you coming for breakfast?"

"Sure! I mean, yes, thank you."

WHILE THEY HEADED across the field and down through the woods to Cherie's house, Samantha asked about the hen fight. "Hey, was the cat hurt? That's a pretty mean chicken."

"Oh, that cat is Gerald. He fights with Miss Betty all the time. And she always wins. He'll never learn to leave her alone. All the other hens will go back inside to bed as soon as the sun goes down. But not Miss Betty. We're not sure where she sleeps, but we're always finding eggs in weird places. If you find one, don't eat it. It coulda been there for months."

"Does Gerald live at your house, or should I be feeding him?"

"He was born at my house, but he adopted Bama, and he hangs out there. I think he's not sure what to do now without her."

"Neither am I," offered Samantha, "but if he comes around, I'll try and make friends with him."

Suddenly the little girl stopped, turned around and stared at Samantha. "Mom said you have red hair. That's not red."

"It was really red when I was little, but as I got older, it got darker. They call it auburn."

"Auburn! Pfft!" the girl huffed. "They should call it Rusty Water Pipe."

They arrived at the back porch steps, and the little girl pointed at the door. "Go on in the kitchen. Tell mom I'll be in in a minute."

"Hey, I forget your name," Sam called after her.

"Anna"

"Hi. I'm Samantha."

"Be a Cherry," Anna called over her shoulder and headed into the back of the garage.

SAM PEERED through the screen door into the kitchen that had changed a little since she was running in and out of here as a child. The duck theme wallpaper had been replaced by a gentle pastel plaid. And she remembered that the cabinets had been all white metal, but she liked these dark wooden ones better.

"Hellooo, Cherie. It's Samantha."

"Come in! Please! Come give me a hug. It's been ages. Now stand still a minute. If I get you at just the right spot, I'll be able to see you.

"There now. You're gorgeous as ever!" She hugged her old childhood friend. Years had passed since they'd spent much time together.

"And you!" said Sam. "You look 20 years old, with your same curly ponytail."

"Well, I'm sure the black has some gray around the edges. I tried short hair for a while. I thought it would be easier to care for, but not when you can't see which parts are sticking out! So I let it grow out again. The ponytail works."

"I gather you've met Anna."

"Yeah. Since Bama was spending every winter in California, I rarely got back here to Maine. So, I missed Anna growing up. In my mind she's still a baby. But why did she tell me to "be a cherry?""

Cherie laughed. "She has a 'learn Italian' tape. It's not 'be a cherry,' but it sounds like something that means 'pleased to meet you.' She gets a kick out of surprising people."

"That explains the Tom Brady tutu."

Cherie put her head between her hands and chuckled. "Oh, that girl! I can't see what she's wearing, so she gets away with a lot. Her reputation at school is nerd, geek, weirdo, loser. I don't know what they call them these days, but she embraces whatever label they saddle her with, and then she feeds it."

"Wait. They have nerds and geeks in elementary school? I thought that was an invention of teenagers."

"She was nicknamed 'Annabutt' in preschool for some inexplicable reason. Maybe 'butt' was the only 'bad' word anyone knew."

"Yeah," agreed Samantha. 'Butt' and 'poop' are pretty handy swear words at that age. But, wow! It has been ages since we've seen each other. I get that Anna's not a baby anymore, but I didn't think she'd be so..."

"So bossy?" offered Cherie with a laugh. "Well, since my sight's pretty much gone, she has a lot of responsibility. Probably too much, but it can't be helped. Nelson is out on the road a lot. He drives for Crawford Transport. I've started the process of getting a guide dog, but that will take a while.

"Anyway, Anna has been looking after the chickens since Bama started forgetting they were out there. And the garlic won't require much till the end of July."

"Oh yes, the garlic," Sam replied with a start. "I hope I can remember what to do. I do remember that we don't pull it up; we dig and lift."

"Right! But don't worry, Sam. I know how to help harvest it. And so does Anna. We got this. We won't let it rot in the ground."

"Cherie, can I ask you something before Anna comes back in?"

"Sure."

"I can't remember the name of your eye disease. When we were 12, you wore glasses, and I remember that you could not see the stars at night. We had talked about how they expected your sight to get worse. Help me understand. Will you lose it completely?"

"It's called retinitis pigmentosa. It's a hereditary disease that's pretty prevalent among the French Acadians. It's in my family and in Nelson's. So, we got Anna tested as soon as she was born."

"They're sure Anna will get it? Does she know?"

"Oh yes. We wouldn't keep a thing like that from her. She's quite pragmatic and eager to learn everything she can while her sight is good. She aces anything she's presented with at school. That's the benefit of early testing. We've had time to prepare for whatever may come. And as for me, at this point, if the light is right, I can see a small area directly in front of me...like looking through a straw. I can read if I hold the paper very close to my eyes in just the right spot. But it's quite tiring."

Then Cherie changed the subject. "I'm making waffles. You want some?"

"Certainly. And sorry, but please tell me how you can make waffles if you can't see?"

Cherie smiled. "I can do a lot of things you might not expect. And my waffle education was not without a few burned fingers in the beginning. But we keep everything in exactly the same place so I can find it. I DO make a mess sometimes!"

"Yes, you do!" said Anna through the screen. She started to open the door but Cherie stopped her with one word, "Boots!"

Anna kicked her boots off in the entryway and came through the door. "I LOVE waffles, so I don't care if I have to clean up mom's messes."

Cherie got a carton of eggs from the fridge.

"I hope you don't mind; we've been using the eggs that don't sell right away."

Samantha shrugged. "Of course not. Someone has to use them. And if you are caring for the chickens, it should be you. Though come to think of it, if you have any to spare, I should take some back over with me. I haven't even turned on the electricity yet. There's nothing in the fridge."

Anna jumped up and scurried into another room, returning a minute later holding a tin canister that sported Star Trek characters.

"Here's the farmstand money."

Sam shook her head.

"No, please keep it. If you've been operating the stand, keep the money!"

Cherie said, "But you don't understand. It's over $300."

"What? Just from eggs?"

"Well, eggs and the peas came up early this year. They have been the proverbial 'hotcakes' so far,"

Anna said, "We were sad about Bama, so we planted her seeds. The tomatoes and zucchini aren't ready yet. Oh! And you're almost out of chicken feed. I can show you where the feed store is."

"Good enough, Anna! I have to get groceries later today, and we can get chicken feed, too. I'll be glad for the company. But, really, keep the money. Put it in your college fund. Or buy yourself a new tutu. That one probably has chicken poop on it."

Anna stood up and turned it around on her waist, looking for barnyard evidence. "No, it doesn't! Just some straw and stuff."

"It's the 'stuff' I was wondering about," said Sam.

The inspection was suddenly abandoned when Cherie announced that the first waffle was coming right up. They soon settled into breakfast with orange juice fresh from the carton and puddles of maple syrup.

AFTERWARD, Sam went back up to Bama's house through what had always been called the woods path. In reality, 'the woods' was just a strip of trees along the Pelletier's backyard. That path had always been there, even when Cherie's grandparents, the Bouchards, lived there. When they were kids, she and Cherie had worn it down to bare earth.

As young children they'd called that 'the little woods.' They weren't ever allowed in 'the big woods,' which is what they called the forest up behind Bama's house. But those few spruce trees had provided plenty of adventure for preschoolers.

The woods path led uphill to the field owned by Bama, where she had her vegetable garden, the raised beds, and the hen house. In the field, Sam hung a left and passed the chickens to arrive in the driveway where her car was parked. She brought her suitcase in and located the electrical panel in the cellar stairway. Then she looked about the kitchen for a coffee maker.

No Keurig and no Mr. Coffee, but she did find Bama's ancient French press and a grinder. Coffee beans sat in a canister beside the stove, just where Sam knew they would be.

Typical Bama, thought Sam.

She would not have bought a Keurig, if only because everyone else in the world used one. She also insisted that she would be the last person on earth to have a social media account, and she probably had been.

While the coffee was brewing, Sam wandered through the house that had once been her home. Much was different, but surprisingly, many things remained the same: things that were part of Bama's personality and not just décor. Like that turtle, carved from desert sandstone, that had always presided over the kitchen from the windowsill above the sink.

Sam tried to remember where that had come from. *I think it was from her friend across the road*, Sam thought. *Donna? No, Diana.*

There was some reason that this little turtle was so precious, but Sam could not remember ever hearing the whole story. When pressed, her grandmother always just said, "That's been here as long as you have."

And the books! Samantha took her time perusing the bookcase. Here was a new group: *The Cost of Discipleship, Surprised By Hope, A Shepherd Looks at Psalm 23, What's So Amazing about Grace?* And a bunch of others, all containing a faith theme. Whenever Bama developed a new interest, she dove into it big time. But a lot of the older books were still there.

In fact, here was the *Gregg Shorthand Manual Simplified*. Sam laughed out loud. She and Cherie had decided to study shorthand so they would have a secret language. They weren't very good at follow-through, or maybe that manual wasn't simplified enough for 10-year-olds. *We would have been better served by learning Braille*, thought Samantha grimly.

And here was *Sister Wendy's Story of Painting*. Sam had another copy in California with her school supplies. But this was the original book that Bama gave her when she was 9 years old. Sister Wendy was not only a nun, but also an art history expert.

Samantha remembered how this book introduced her to all the different approaches to painting since the cave people. It also turned out to be a fairly complete sex education for a nine-yr.-old. And fairly confusing, as well. Cherie and I thought it was ridiculous to see a whole group of people at a picnic in old-fashioned clothes, with a naked woman just sitting there on the ground. She looked totally unaware that she had no clothes on.

Then there was the lady fully dressed in a long gown

sitting in her living room with one boob sticking out. *That looked really silly,* Sam had thought. *And what happened to Baby Jesus' swaddling clothes? In every picture of him, he was naked or very nearly. In December!*

All the naked men looked pretty much the same "down there," so when she was a kid, she figured that was what all men must look like. Sam remembered asking Bama if that was the case. Her grandmother had looked over and said, "Yep, pretty much."

Sam shifted her gaze and her thoughts to what had apparently become the cookbook shelf (not to be confused with the organic gardening shelf, or the books about foods and chemicals to avoid shelf, or the how to improve your health shelf). She pulled out a well-worn little book called *200 Jams and Preserves.* It had full color photos on the right hand pages opposite the recipes on the left. As she flipped through it, she noticed many of the pages bore evidence of hard usage.

"Bama, what's Chutney?"

"That's like a jam with lots of chunks in it and not always sweet," she answered.

"Well, who in the world could stand to eat Green Bean Chutney?"

Bama took the book and looked at the page I had open. "Even if you hate green beans, you may like that. It's got lots of onions and vinegar. I think you're the only kid in the state who will eat onions and vinegar. I have to stop you from drinking the juice straight out of the pickle jar, for heaven's sake!"

"That's just because you've been feeding me garlic since I was a baby. I think you put it in my formula!"

"I never!" insisted Bama. "It was just always on my hands. A person's sense of smell gets all mixed up with their sense of taste.

Anyway, look in that book and see if they've got any peas or broc-coli chutney, and we'll give it a try."

———————

SAMANTHA SMILED TO HERSELF. It's true: the smell of garlic had always been strangely nostalgic and comforting to her. Also true: she still drank the pickle juice straight from the jar. And she hated green beans. But Bama had eventually pickled some beans with dill and onions. She'd have a look around and see if there was still a jar of those somewhere.

So strange to be here, thought Samantha, *oddly familiar and yet oddly unfamiliar all at the same time. And to think that this book, this turtle, some random jar of pickled green beans—that all these things belong to me.*

She had to decide what to do with the remains of Bama's life. The will stated, "All my earthly belongings I bequeath to my granddaughter Samantha Erin Sullivan because she is fair, generous, and sensible."

Sam pondered that for a moment. *Bama may have thought I was all those things, but I still don't know what to do.*

She poured herself a cup of coffee, slumped into the sofa, and surrendered to a boisterous, sobbing cry.

CHAPTER TWO

*S*am spent the rest of that day and most of the next getting settled in, getting herself reaccustomed to her surroundings. She stocked the refrigerator, and called for propane to be delivered so she could cook; but mostly, she sat on the porch, inhaling the perfume from the lilacs lining one side of the driveway. Eventually, she decided to tackle Bama's bedroom.

Two hours later, she sat on the hardwood floor surrounded by papers and boxes. The bed itself had also disappeared under piles of things that had to be sorted before she could sleep in here. At first, Sam had thought that sleeping in this bed would make her feel even more sad about losing Bama. But two nights on the sofa had convinced her to seek out a more permanent arrangement. She was beginning to realize that this chore could take weeks.

For now, though, Sam decided to just leave everything where it was. She ventured upstairs to her childhood bedroom, curious about how that might have changed. It had become more like an office, although it still had a bed and a dresser. Her mother's high school picture was on the shelf above the dresser, where it had always been.

The quilt on the bed was the one that Bama had helped her make when she was 10 years old. Black around the edges, then dark blue, fading into lighter and lighter shades of blue, and then white in the center. Sam had always loved looking at that from across the room. It was a little sun-faded on the side by the window, but not too bad. This was going home with her.

In the closet, there was a plastic tote filled with all her old sketchbooks. Bama had labeled them all with Sam's name and age when she finished each one. These were full of memories she would savor on some rainy day, when she was tucked up beside the woodstove. Her little desk that Bama had let her paint with pond lilies back when she was a child was now piled with file folders and small boxes.

Sam opened one of the boxes and found the labels that Bama used to mail garlic to her customers. The words "Royalty Garlic" surrounded the logo that Samantha had designed herself: a chubby, smiling bulb of garlic, wearing a golden crown.

"WELL, of course she's wearing a crown, Bama! She's from Royalty, Maine! Get it?"

"It's perfect, Sammi! It's very handy to have an artist in the family."

"Do you think I AM an artist?"

"Yes, I do. Just keep sketching and experimenting, and seeing, and you'll get better and better."

"But what do you mean, 'keep seeing.' Of course, I will keep seeing, Bama!"

"Well, what I mean is...well, like this:"

Bama pointed to a calendar with photos of ocean life. "Look at this whale jumping out of the water. What color is he?"

"Gray"

"What color is the water?"

"Blue"

"And the sky?"

"Light blue"

"Now, this time don't think about whales and the water and the sky. Just look at the blotches of color. What colors can you pick out?"

"Ok. Well, there's gray, of course, and black and white and lots of different shades of blue and white and little tiny bits of green... and... pink! There's little tiny sparkles of pink and brown... and gold!"

"Being able to see all that is what makes you an artist! Soon you'll look at things and find layers of color, shapes within shapes, and shadows behind shadows. Keep seeing, not just looking. Remember this: The most obvious thing is usually not the whole thing. There's always something more."

SAMANTHA REFLECTED upon her grandmother's advice. It had served her well throughout her education and life. Maybe she would make herself some sort of a framed quote, and credit Bama's name at the bottom. "The most obvious thing is usually not the whole thing." Or, "Keep looking, keep seeing...there's always something more." Nancy Noreen Sullivan.

Sam had learned to see a lot of what was behind the obvious. It had helped her survive the move to California and learn to love her mother. And it certainly had made her a better teacher.

Her middle schoolers showed up in her art classes, some

with innate talent, some with none. But all of them needed someone to encourage them through the murk of adolescence and help them see a little better. She loved her job and loved her students. They all made her heart ache.

But right now, she needed to massage the ache that the loss of Bama had left.

So Sam made some coffee in the kitchen, took a mug out onto the porch, and then settled into one of the ancient Adirondack chairs that sat exactly where they had always been. These chairs are pretty and quaint. You can ease into them effortlessly, and you can sit comfortably for hours. But you can't get out of them! At least not gracefully, and not while holding a mug of hot coffee. So, she settled in for the duration.

From this low-slung position, Sam had an unbroken view under the railing and down the driveway. To her surprise, she saw a car coming up the driveway, an image that flipped her back to another time, and another car—one that had changed everything.

I WAS out on the porch, finishing up a piece of my birthday cake. I had just turned twelve on Sunday. It was unusually hot for early June; the ice cream I had plopped on top of the cake had already melted.

"Bama, someone's coming up the driveway. It's a taxi! Who would take a taxi to our house?"

Bama appeared at the kitchen door, drying her hands. The taxi stopped, and the driver popped the trunk.

After a minute, a beautiful young blonde got out of the car. She was tall and thin like Bama and her frosted hair was pulled back from her face with a big butterfly clip. She tugged on her skinny jeans, adjusted her tank top, and shouldered a large purse. Then she went around to get a shiny pink suitcase from the back. She slammed the trunk and slapped twice on the roof of the taxi. The driver turned and headed down the driveway.

Bama said, "Michelle?"

The woman answered "Surprise! It really is me." I stood up, and the woman stopped in her tracks and looked at me. "Samantha?"

I could hardly breathe, but I hesitated for just a split second, then said, "Surprise! It really is me!"

Bama laughed but the woman just kept staring at me. "Wow. You sure have grown up while I was away."

I said, "And you still look exactly like your high school picture in my room." I desperately wanted to get to know this beautiful lady who had written to me now and then since before I could read. Some of her letters expressed her sorrow that she'd had that accident while I was only weeks old… before she got a chance to raise me. Her words were always filled with promise for when we could at last be together. I dearly loved Bama, but maybe now I could have a real mother like everyone else. I almost ran down off the porch to hug her.

But my mother said, "You got any coffee?"

Bama nodded and motioned her up the steps. I abandoned my cake and ice cream and we went into the house. Michelle set her suitcase down and gave Bama an awkward little shoulder hug. Bama poured some coffee. And then we sat in the kitchen and basically stared at each other. It was hard to grasp that this stranger was actually my mother!

Finally, she said, "Sorry I haven't written in a while. I actually could write more often while I was in prison...but do me a favor, please? When we talk about the time I was away, let's call it college. Let's say I was away at college. Because it was an education for real! I learned an awful lot while I was in there."

I nodded and stared at the table. Bama said, "We got your last letter about planning a cross country trip. Tell us more about what you're thinking."

My mother proceeded to tell us about taking an HVAC course in prison, and then when she was on work-release she did sales for a heat pump and air-conditioner company. She had to go right back to the group home after work, but that gave her a chance to save most of her paycheck. They wouldn't let her go out and work in people's houses, but at least the course gave her what she needed to know when she was talking to customers in the showroom. Now, she said, she was ready to "move on."

"What do you mean?" I asked her, worried she was leaving again.

"Oh, I just mean I've worked hard to save enough for a real vacation...a road trip, and I want you to come along." She was looking at me.

I shot a plea towards Bama. "Can I? Can I go with her? Cherie and I were going to start Karate this summer, but this is way better. I never thought I'd have the chance to take a road trip. And we can get to know each other!"

Bama managed a smile. "Well, school's out and she IS your mother."

Then Bama looked over at her daughter. " I really wish we had had more notice...but legally, the judge only granted me temporary custody while you were...unavailable."

I piped right up, "You mean while she was in college, right?"

"Right," said Bama and my mother both at once.

BUT THAT WAS A LIFETIME AGO. Now, Sam turned her attention to the Subaru Forester that had pulled up the driveway. The driver parked, turned off the engine and got out.

"Hi, are you Samantha?" The older man seemed very familiar to her, but she could not quite place him. She struggled up out of the Adirondack chair and went down the steps to meet him.

"Yes, Hi, Samantha Sullivan.

"Ted Weller" the man said, extending his hand, "from across the road. Do you remember me?"

"Of course! Mr. Weller!" Sam shook his hand. She remembered now that Ted had had a huge tangle of dark brown curls...but his hair was much straighter now, thinner, shorter and pure white. "You always plowed our driveway. I suppose it's you that's been mowing our lawn.

Ted nodded and Sam thanked him. "And I remember Diana. She was Bama's pickle-making friend. How is she?"

"She doesn't make pickles anymore, but she'd love to sit and talk about your grandmother when, or if, you've got the time. She's having a hard job to get over losing her good friend."

"I'm having a hard time, too," said Samantha. "I would enjoy talking to her, thank you."

"Well, she naps in the afternoons, but any morning just drop on over for coffee."

"Would tomorrow be too soon? Maybe 10 o'clock? I can bring muffins."

"Sounds perfect. I'll let her know to expect you. Anyway, I just brought you Nancy's car. Here are the keys. The registration's in the glove compartment; good till December."

Sam was a little confused. "Why was her car at your place? I was thinking she might have sold it."

Ted tried to explain, "Well, when she didn't go out to California this winter like she had been, I took the car for an oil change; and as the months passed by, no one wanted her to drive, but we could not bear to report her to the DMV. I did get the oil changed, actually; it just happened to take six months! Every time I told her I'd have it back in a few days, either she pretended to be unaware, or she really didn't notice how much time had passed, but she'd say, 'Well, OK then.'

"And we made sure she wasn't house-bound; we picked her up and took her everywhere with us." He sighed and shook his head a little.

Sam remembered that Bama and Diana had folded laundry at the homeless shelter every Monday for years. And the church seemed to have a lot going on, so she would have had lots of people contact. But she wished someone had called her to tell her the truth about Bama's condition.

"Anyway, the car is yours." Ted said. Then he waved his hand toward the Chevy she'd driven up from Boston. "Is that one a rental?"

"Yeah. I can call and have them come pick it up. Thank you so much for looking after her. I didn't have any real idea how quickly her dementia was progressing. I just noticed on the phone that she was very vague and repeated herself a lot."

"No problem. For sure, it was a quick decline, but there were a lot of us keeping an eye on her. What are friends for, right?"

Mr. Weller walked back down the driveway toward his house which Samantha couldn't really see from where she was standing, because of the trees. She watched until he disappeared around the corner.

She was excited at the prospect of some time with Diana. Talking to someone who had known Bama and who had known her mother could clear up many of the questions Sam still had; things her mother told her that she needed to confirm. Diana, at least, will have another side to the story that will help her settle some things in her head.

THE NEXT MORNING, Sam held the sandstone turtle in both hands and eased him down into the basket which she had lined with some paper towels.

She carefully put a dish towel and the plastic container of supermarket muffins on top of the turtle, then set off down the hill to have a chat with Diana.

Diana melted a little when she saw the turtle, sat down and stroked it lovingly. "Yes, I gave that to her. Thank you so much for bringing it back."

"Will you tell me the story behind it?" ventured Samantha. "Bama would only ever say that it came from Mexico."

"Yes, it did. I brought it home in my suitcase for her."

Diana poured two mugs of coffee, and arranged the muffins on a small plate. She handed Sam a cloth napkin embroidered with bright red cardinals. "While I was in Mexico, I passed this little turtle every day. The artisan had it sitting right at eye level, and it had such a grim expression I felt it needed a home. I knew it belonged on your grandmother's kitchen windowsill."

"What were you doing in Mexico?" asked Sam.

"Nancy and I were both planning to go. Not for a vacation, but to help this mission that we support. They do a week-long outreach to the really poor neighborhoods and the red-light district...hand out bags of groceries and clothing...and they put the volunteers up in a dormitory at an orphanage they run. Three days before we were to leave... you showed up."

"That's when I was born?"

"No, you were about two weeks old. Your mother arrived on the back of a motorcycle. No one knew you existed until your mother showed us what was tucked up under her jacket, bound against her chest."

Samantha's birth certificate said she was born in Newark,

New Jersey and there was no father listed. She'd never had any more information than that.

"Michelle had taken off with a boyfriend in the middle of her senior year. Nancy didn't know where she was, or what had happened to her, and the police had no luck finding her. Your grandmother didn't hear a word from her until the following summer when she came back home...plus one.

"I was over at your place having tea. We heard a throbbing motorcycle pull into the yard. We both rushed out the door and onto the porch to see a Harley, driven by a huge guy complete with a ponytail, tattoos and a faded bandana. Michelle, your mom, got off the back. She was wearing a big stuffed backpack, and of course the bulge under the front of her jacket that turned out to be you.

"We asked who the guy was, but your mom said she didn't know. He was just a guy who gave her a ride up from Portland. So, we both assumed that Portland was where she had been.

"She wouldn't say where she'd been for the last year, what her plans were, or if she had made any. She was just here, and you were here. Nancy warmed up something for her to eat, and Michelle pulled some powdered formula out of her backpack, spooned some into an empty bottle and filled it at the kitchen sink. She asked me if I wanted to feed you.

"I held you and your bottle for a few minutes. Then Nancy insisted I hand you over. She said she needed a closer look at her new granddaughter. We fussed over you and Michelle went to take a shower.

"The next morning Nancy called the Bouchards next door to you. Their daughter and son-in-law lived with them and had a baby about 3 months old...that was Cherie... and your Bama was able to borrow some outgrown baby clothes and a little folding bed.

"Nancy canceled her travel plans, and I left for a week in

Mexico. One morning just before I got back, Nancy woke up to hear you crying." Diana stopped. "I'm sorry, dear, you might not want to hear this part."

"No, Please go on. I don't trust anything my mother ever told me. It's about time I heard the truth."

"Ok then," said Diana gently, "When you didn't stop crying, Nancy went upstairs to the little bedroom, and discovered that Michelle and her backpack were gone. No note. Just gone. For weeks no one knew where she'd gone or how she managed it. Nancy informed the police that she was missing, but because of her age, I don't think they looked very hard."

The silence hung heavily in the air, until Samantha pressed for more, "And then?"

Diana sighed. "Nancy got a visit from the state police. They told her that Michelle had stolen a car, driven it to North Carolina and while she was drunk, caused an accident that killed 3 people. The car had been reported stolen, but they weren't looking in North Carolina, so it took a while to put the facts together."

Samantha was stunned. "Wow! Mom didn't talk about it much, but when I asked her why she went to prison, she would only say she was in an accident, and they blamed it on her. But where did she get the car?"

Diana looked down and picked at the placemat. "From our driveway." Then she looked up quickly. "I'm so sorry. The car was totaled, but the insurance replaced it, and there was no point in our being angry." Then she laughed. "But we did stop leaving the keys in the ashtray!"

Samantha felt the disappointment physically. Just like every time her mother had let her down. When she was twelve, that gut punch had sent her running to the bathroom, but it had grown less severe over the years. Now it was merely a familiar sinking feeling.

Sam reminded Diana that when her mother was released from prison, their "road trip" had turned out to be an underhanded way to get Sam to move to California; her mother's plan all along. She refused to take Sam back to Maine. These days, once in a while Sam would run into someone who asked about Michelle Sullivan, wondering if they were related. She didn't always admit it. She'd usually say something like, "There are an awful lot of Sullivans in this country. None left in Ireland apparently."

But this was just one more piece that explained a lot of her childhood and adolescence. She hadn't known her mother had just abandoned her as an infant. But she was not surprised; because it happened again when Sam turned 18.

The day of her birthday, their landlords, Mr. and Mrs. Springer, showed up at her door with a birthday cake, a half-gallon of ice cream, and a new pair of jeans wrapped in gold paper! They sang, Sam blew out the candles and they ate. Two days later, she woke up to find that her mother and her clothes were gone. No note. Just gone.

That morning, while pondering what might have become of her mother, she ate the last piece of cake for breakfast. Then she went across the breezeway to see Mrs. Springer, because by that time, they had become good friends.

They talked about whether Sam's mom might come back, and what she should do. Mrs. Springer's advice was to keep on with what Sam had already planned to do, which was to go to Valley Community College, and get her core classes out of the way cheaply. Then transfer to Cal State Northridge, for art education.

The Springers allowed her to continue living there in the guest house, rent-free so long as Sam was in school, and kept the yardwork caught up.

"So that's what I did." Sam told Diana. "And as time went on, the Springers got older and frailer, and relied on me more and more. So, I stayed, graduated and have been working ever since teaching art in the Los Angeles Unified School District.

"I think it was about a year after my mom left; I had just started my sophomore year in college, Mr. Springer died. I knew it was vital that I stay there right next door to Mrs. Springer and take on more of the things like hauling trash cans, and doing the grocery shopping that he used to do.

"Then I got a postcard from Las Vegas. 'Hope you are doing well. I'm having a blast. Michelle.' I never heard from her or saw her alive again after that."

WHEN I HAD to identify her body in the morgue, it was hard to be sure at first.

She was laying on a high bed in a tiny room. There was a window from the hallway, in case you didn't want to go inside. The detective asked me which I wanted to do, and I told him I needed to see her up close. But she was hard to look at. They had her covered up to her neck and there was a scarf over part of her face and head. The part of her face that I could see was bruised.

The officer put his hand gently on my back and said that her boyfriend had done this to her, and that they had him in custody. The way he said that one word, "boyfriend," with a sardonic little twist to it, dissuaded me from asking any questions. I said I did remember that her eyebrows had that crooked little arch, but to be sure, I asked to see her left hand.

He pulled the sheet up to her wrist. The little finger on this purplish left hand was perfectly formed, but only came just past the first knuckle on her ring finger. Her nail polish was lovely, but the nail itself was broken off. That short little finger confirmed it was her.

My mother never did have great taste in men. I didn't want to think about how she might have ended up in this condition.

———

SAM PULLED her mind back into the present moment here with Diana. She found a tissue in her pocket and blew her nose.

Diana sat in the silence with her for a minute, and then spoke very quietly. "I'm so sorry, dear. I'm sure it was a difficult time. But Nancy was very much a part of the church by the time your mother died. And we were all praying for you both while she was out there to help you bury Michelle.

"Your Bama was only gone for three or four days, if I remember correctly, and she didn't have a whole lot to say when she came back. She just got busy planting garlic. It was a little earlier than she typically would have done that, but I'm sure it was therapeutic for her."

"For sure," said Sam, absentmindedly. This visit with Diana had produced a lot of information and stirred up so many conflicting emotions. She needed to be alone for a while. She asked Diana to excuse her and gave her a hug. She stood up slowly, picked up her empty basket, said a sincere "thank you", and crossed the road.

When she returned to the house, she could not face the mountain of chores waiting for her. So instead, she decided to go check out the raised bed that held the garlic crop. Maybe she'd even locate Gerald the cat and chase the chickens with him. Some activity would be good.

She passed the chickens fussing about in their run. Gerald was nowhere to be found. So, she set out across the field to look at the garlic crop.

Sam was astonished to find not three raised beds, but twelve! Four of them were just empty boxes, with no soil.

Another four held peas and tomatoes, cucumbers and zucchini. But the four closest to her all had evenly spaced green garlic tops stretching skyward. How could she have missed this when she crossed this field that first morning?

Sam noticed a large metal number 3 on the edge of the raised bed she was standing beside. "They're numbered," she observed aloud.

"Yes they are," said Cherie's voice behind her. She and Anna joined her beside the garlic beds.

"Nelson put those on for me this spring. They're all on the end that faces the house. It helps me orient myself. And there are wind chimes marking the woods path. I use my cane so I don't trip. It's a slow process, but I can actually come up here by myself, if I need to."

"Oh dear!" Sam said.. "What am I going to do with all this garlic? There must be hundreds!"

"Twelve hundred thirty-six," said Cherie. "A lot of that is already promised to Bama's regulars. You just have to locate her list."

Sam sputtered, "Good Grief! Do I mail all this?"

"No," said Anna. "Lots of her customers live around here. You have to call them and they'll come over. Anyway, not yet. Do you know how to tell when they're ready?"

"Uhhhh…" Sam studied the garden for a minute. "Yeah, sure! The leaves need to start to die."

"But not completely dead brown," added Anna. "The very bottom leaves start to turn yellow, see? Then, we need to wait for a few more leaves to turn yellow, and then a couple days of no rain."

Cherie added, "The entire plant has to be laid out to dry. Then they are trimmed and the bulbs have to be sorted and laid out to cure."

"I remember that part well enough," said Samantha. "It used to be my job to lay it all out in the attic of the shed. And it was a picky job! She was very fussy about how that garlic was handled."

"Yep" said Cherie. " When you left, I was pretty much underfoot all the time anyway, so Bama gave that job to me. In recent years, it's been Anna's.

"We've tried drying it in other places. But that shed is really the best. It's hot and dry with no sun, and there's a breeze blowing through from one end to the other all the time. It's perfect."

Samantha continued to gaze at the rows of raised beds. They were all about three feet high, just the perfect height to sit on and work in the soil. "Who built all this? Are these railroad ties?"

"No!" exclaimed Cherie. "Railroad ties are soaked with creosote so they don't rot. But that's not something you want in your food. Anyway, my man, Nelson, built these. Anna says her Dad can build anything, and I think she's right.

"His job takes him all over the state, and once, he passed a place where they were tearing down a barn. They had already sold a lot of the bigger beams, but they let him have the smaller ones and the damaged ones just for hauling them away. He brought them back here when his truck was otherwise empty, and spent the better part of last summer building these beds."

"Oh yes," Sam remembered. "Bama told me on the phone about new beds. But the details weren't clear. I figured she was talking about what she planned, or wanted to do, or she even might have been talking about furniture. I really didn't expect this!"

Cherie and Anna were beaming. "She was so looking forward to planting the new beds. We helped her put this garlic in last fall. There's enough to keep her regular customers coming, but she wanted to go big, and do more mail orders. So sad to lose her."

"Well," said Sam. "Her customer list is probably in the little desk, upstairs in what used to be my bedroom."

"The pond lily desk?" exclaimed Anna. "I love that desk! It looks exactly like the pond down by the farmstand...in the fog."

"Yep" agreed Sam, "For most of my childhood, I was obsessed with how things looked through the fog. It took years, but I finally discovered how to paint fog and mist and smoke. And, you can't really tell, but underneath that lily pond is about 15 layers of paint. Your mom and I were always coming up with something new and different."

"Right!" agreed Cherie. "Do you remember the black with stars and comets...what did we call it...Galaxy something?"

"Galactic!" said Sam. "Galactic Sojourn!"

Cherie laughed. "You're right! Where did we get that? We were pretty big for our britches, weren't we?"

"Right! That wasn't my favorite, though...no fog in outer space!"

Cherie and Anna got busy picking peas. Sam offered to help, but they refused. "I know you have a ton to do over at the house. You're just looking for an excuse to play in the garden."

RIGHT NOW, Sam thought as she wandered back across the lawn, *Oh man. Right now, I need to clear up the fog in my head and my heart, and get a plan in place at least.*

But that afternoon, and for the next three days, she mostly sat on the porch.

She stared out the window at the rain for hours one cold morning, then built a fire in the woodstove and stared through the glass at the flames for the whole afternoon.

The next day, she wandered through the house, picking

up one thing after another and putting it down again. Once she scooped up all the jackets and coats in the entryway, and piled them on the sofa. She stared at the heap for a few minutes. This was not progress.

Sam could not focus on any task. She had supposed that being busy with material things would help her process her grief, but it felt more like her grief was getting in the way of everything else.

Finally, in frustration, Samantha forced herself to sit at the kitchen table with a pen and a pad of paper.

1. Decide what I want to keep.

2. Decide what to do with the rest.

"There. There's a plan!"

She moved a chair out of the corner of the living room and designated that six square feet of empty floor as her space for things she wanted to keep. In the middle of that space she put the 200 Jams and Preserves book. Then she stood and stared at the floor and the book.

Sam wandered out onto the porch and sat down. Sunk into the Adirondack chair, she gazed at what she could see of the bright blue sky glimpsed through the dark green pines. Brilliant chartreuse new growth showed on the end of each branch, and seagulls circled so high they were just sparkles of white as the sun reflected off their wings.

A hummingbird buzzed past her, and headed for the feeder on the end of the porch.

"Thank you, Lord, for hummingbirds and pine trees and seagulls," she said out loud, glad that she'd had the presence of mind to fill the feeders.

Her thoughts stormed all over the place, between what Diana had told her about her mother, what to do with Bama's jackets, and how beautiful and calm it was here in this chair. She tried to direct her prayers heavenward, past the pines, past the seagulls.

The conflict in Sam's head consumed her. *A lot is being required of me, and I'm not prepared. I really don't know how to proceed. I just want to sit here in this chair and not move. I loved Bama so much. I love this place and I never want to leave, but at the same time, I love my life back home. 'Please, Jesus, show me what to do.'*

She was just about to surrender to another crying spell, when her phone rang. It was Cherie.

"Hey," she said. "Nelson and Anna have taken off to the supermarket. They always turn it into an hours-long adventure. So, why don't you come over? We'll have some lunch and a real talk. I think that's something you need."

At the kindness and insight of her friend, Sam burst into tears.

CHAPTER THREE

*S*am and Cherie finished their sandwiches and popped the paper plates into the trash. Sam wiped her mouth and picked a cherry tomato out of the bowl in the middle of the table.

"I didn't think you would have ripe tomatoes so early."

"Oh," explained Cherie, "those are from Anna's greenhouse."

"Her greenhouse?"

"Yeah, you must have seen it, behind the garage? We thought she'd be more likely to eat fresh veggies if she grew them herself. Tomatoes and peppers are really good to improve eye health, but they don't grow very early in Maine. So, a couple years ago, we got her that little greenhouse. Most of those cherry tomatoes don't make it into the house, 'cause she eats them too fast."

"What are they saying about her eyes at this point," asked Sam?

"Well, we've always known she carries the gene, but it's not really possible to predict how or when, or to what degree it will manifest itself. So, we determined when she was just a baby that we would give her the best possible nutrition and the best preparation. And she goes once a year for a complete work-up…she'll go more often if and when symptoms start."

Cherie explained that they do not use anything that comes ready to eat in a package. They eat a lot of eye-healthy vegetables, eggs and fish. In fact, when Anna was little, they'd had a color chart on the fridge and she was supposed to eat 3 different colors each day and mark it on the chart.

"I've had countless people tell me, 'Oh you can't cure RP with diet!'

"My answer to that is: no one's ever tried it from birth onward. Well, perhaps it won't cure it, but there is some thought that certain vitamins will slow the progression. Anyway, it was a fun way to learn colors, and we're all way healthier than we would have been otherwise."

Cherie told her friend that just last year Anna was put into a 7-year clinical study that's looking at the benefit of micronutrients instead of standard vitamin supplements. All the participants were under age eight at the start, all have the inherited gene. They figure they'll be able to see a difference by the end of the study, because puberty is about when the disease kicks in if it's going to. Anna was placed in one of the groups that has to pay attention to diet, but, of course, they won't know if she's taking the placebo or the real supplements until the study is completed.

Sam wondered, "Does she feel like she misses out on treats?"

"She doesn't miss all that much. We work hard to find alternative snacks that are tasty. She carries her lunch to school, and she probably trades for junk food. I don't know. But at home she sticks to the plan pretty well. We never call it a diet.

And she negotiates, as you might imagine. When she was 4, she made the case…and won…that French vanilla ice cream is the same color as the inside of a banana so it counts as a yellow food. We just make sure we get the kind that has real eggs in it, not just food coloring.

The 'Saturday Adventures' that she and Nelson go on started out as a reward for staying faithful to her food plan while he was gone. If she could honestly say she stuck to it, he would take her out for ice cream. Once in kindergarten, she knew she really blew it.

When he got home from his run Friday night, she was in tears because she would miss their outing. But Nelson is pretty wise. He acted really disappointed, then he asked her, 'Do you think it would be cheating if we went and did something else, and just not eat ice cream?' She thought about that a while and then said, 'What would we do?'"

Cherie said that they finally agreed to go roller skating topped off with a veggie pizza. And they still count on spending every Saturday together.

"Well," said Sam. "Speaking of Anna, I wonder if you would care to translate her for me?"

Cherie chuckled. "Do you want the entire Anna, or something specific?"

"Well, she was scolding me for not being able to tell a seed garlic bulb from a kitchen-use bulb. She stopped and stared at me. Then she just said, 'Your eyes don't sparkle.' And walked away."

Cherie responded. "That does not take much translation. Now of course, I can't see it, but I would hear it...and...I don't. Uhhh, no sparkle. So, what's up?"

Samantha stared at the table, with her head in her hands.

Finally she sighed. "I'm stuck! Overwhelmed! I haven't done anything for three days! Yesterday, because it was so cold in the morning, I got the wood stove going, sat and drank coffee and watched the fire for hours. After a while I was practically in a coma, so I ate some yogurt and went to bed. I want to just sit here forever and never do anything."

Cherie reached across the table and Sam took her hand. "Sammi," she said, deliberately reverting to her childhood nickname. "Think of Bama, when she was talking about her flower gardens or her chickens, or her garlic crop. Picture her face."

Sam really wasn't sure what this conversation was about. "Well, the garlic, and the chickens, and her house…it's all so mixed up with my love for Bama. I thought I had done my grieving in March when the weather had me stranded in a Boston hotel, and I missed the funeral. But being here has opened the wound again. I don't think anything would make me 'sparkle' today."

"Fair enough," said Cherie. "I lost both my parents within six months of each other, and I can tell you, it never really goes away. But It does ease up. Someday your memories won't hurt, they will be comforting."

Samantha dug into her pocket and pulled out the paper she'd been working from: her PLAN. She read it aloud to Cherie, "1. Decide what I want to keep. 2. Decide what to do with everything else."

Cherie waited for the rest, but Sam said, "That's all."

"Hmm. Well, good start! They say that planning is 90% of the job. So, let's talk about your options: Garage sales clear out a lot of stuff, but take a huge amount of work on your part. And this really isn't a good location for a sale. Also, if you're going to sell the house you could possibly sell it furnished. Or you could rent it. But I have a friend who owns several rental properties. She says it's constant work for very little profit, and there's always something the tenants are calling you about. To try to manage the property from California would be a challenge for sure."

Sam groaned. "Maybe I'll just stay right here. Then I don't have to make any decisions."

Cherie countered, "Wrong. You'll still have a ton of decisions; you'll have to quit your job, then find a job here, and there is an amazing amount of work to be done when someone dies. And, my dear, you're forgetting the sparkle factor."

Sam groaned again. She got up and reached for the coffee pot. "You want a top up?"

Cherie nodded, and Sam poured.

Sam sat back down and squeezed Cherie's hand as silent tears dripped onto the tablecloth.

Cherie continued, "Sam, you love your memories of this place, and you loved Bama, but you don't want to live her life, do you? Tell me what *do* you love about *your* life?"

Sam blew her nose, cleared her throat and thought a minute.

"OK then. I love California's beaches and the weather: the sunshine in February. I love rollerblading. I love all the different languages and cultures all around me, mixed together, but still unique. I especially love the Hispanic culture. It's so full of color and life and joy. The rest of us just don't know how to celebrate. In fact, I was thinking that when budget cuts happen, which they always do, the art dept is often the first to suffer. Maybe I'll go back to school and get certified in English as a Second Language. There will probably always be a place for that.

"And believe it or not, I love driving on the freeway, especially at night. The 101 is so beautiful with the rows and rows of traffic winding through the hills. I love knowing that I belong to that big picture.

"I love Georgia O'Keefe and her bones and her big, big flowers. They make me believe in a God who created that detail and gave her the gift to replicate it. I love the idea that there are billions of flowers blooming all over the world, that no one ever sees. They could serve the same purpose for bees and birds, if they weren't beautiful to the human eye, but they are!"

Cherie urged her on. "What else?"

Sam thought a minute. "Well, there was a seventh grader last year who actually apologized for being so grumpy. He said he hates art and he can't do it and he was only in my class because he needed to have an elective and chess was full. He complained, 'they let kids in there who don't even know how to play!'

So, we sat down and I asked him to tell me what was cool about chess. He started to tell me about rules and order, and strategy and structure, and yes, his eyes sparkled! He said, 'It's almost as good as math.'

I asked him to stick with me and we would search out the order and symmetry in nature...we would find the art in math and the math in art. I gave him Bama's famous line: 'Look beyond the obvious; there's always something more.'

Well, you should see the stuff he was producing by the end of the year. His masterpiece was a close-up of a sunflower. All math and symmetry, structure, repetition and beautiful art. Very O'Keeffesque, as a matter of fact.

Middle schoolers have such a hard time. Very few of them have any center, any confidence, any semblance of hope. I know how they feel, because I've 'been there and done that'. If I really need to convince them that all is not lost, I tell them my story. When they find out I have no clue who my father is, and my mother spent my whole childhood in prison, I get their attention. Of course, Bama gave me a great start, but when my mom took me, wow. If it hadn't been for the Springers who saw some value in me, I might not have made it through those early days in California.

I love my students, but what I really love is the process of helping them find the beauty in everything around them. The look on their faces when they finally discover what lies beyond the obvious."

Cherie sat back in her chair. "Now we're getting somewhere. I can hear the sparkle. And while I realize you can find students here if you were to stay, all those other things are sort of specific to California, aren't they?"

"Yes, they are," agreed Samantha. "Plus, there's Mrs. Springer. I'm still living in her guest house, although these days I spend more time in her house. Her hips are bad and it hurts her to get around. So, I need to be there."

"Anyone else?" Cherie ventured, "Like a man?"

"Well, there is a man. I wouldn't call him *my* man," Sam hurried to add, "but he's not anyone else's either.

His name is Marshall Mayfield. I've known him since I was in seventh grade, and he was in ninth. His father owned an art supply store in our neighborhood that he named for his son. It's called 'Marshall Arts'. We didn't have too much to do with each other in the beginning, but after school he worked in the shop, and of course I was in and out of there all the time.

When he went off to college, I started working there, and still do on weekends. Marshall came back a couple years ago to take over the store when his father died. His younger brothers are in landscaping and aren't interested in art supplies.

Anyway, he's become a great friend. We spend a lot of time together. He's just a genuinely good man."

"Hmmm," mused Cherie. "Now that kind of sounds like a boyfriend. Does he think of you that way?"

"Funny you should say that. When I left to come here, he asked me to figure out what kind of relationship we have. So, I've got that on my mind as well. And I got the strangest text this morning." Sam pulled out her phone and found the text from Marshall. She read it to Cherie.

"It says '2tim13b4'"

"That's all?" asked Cherie.

"Yep!"

"Do you know what it means?"

"Yes, It's from 2nd Timothy in the New Testament. It says he's praying for me night and day, and longing to see me, so he will be filled with joy!"

Cherie smiled. "Now that does sound like a boyfriend. Did you answer him?"

"Not yet. We said we weren't going to talk till I got back."

"Why was that?"

Sam thought back over her last conversation with Marshall.

ON THE WAY out to the car, Marshall took my arm and held it until I stopped and turned to look at him. "Samantha, let me ask you a question...and please tell me the truth."

"Uhm, OK"

"Do you spend time with me just because I'm safe?"

"What do you mean? I like you and we always do things together! You are for sure, my best friend."

"I know" responded Marshall, "But are we going together? Are we dating?"

"I don't think so," I said. "Dates are usually awkward. But when you and I go somewhere, it feels comfortable and natural."

Marshall nodded. "Hence my question. Do you spend time with me just because I'm safe or, could you love me?"

"Give me a minute to think about that..." But I took 5 minutes, pacing up and down the sidewalk, little finger tapping the entire time, while Marshall stood there looking at the pavement.

Then I said, "Look, I'm leaving tomorrow for Maine. I have a *lot of stuff to deal with back there. Let me give you my answer after I get back. I promise I will give you an honest answer."*

SAM ROUSED herself and addressed Cherie's earlier question about Marshall. "I thought it would be easier to think about how I felt if he wasn't around."

"How's that working for you?"

"Truth is," said Samantha, "I probably depend on him for a lot of things. I'm used to talking things out with him, and afterwards, even when he hasn't said a word, I'm able to make a decision, and then life makes sense again. It's been hard to resist the urge to call him and ask him what I should do."

"Hmmm. Interesting."

"Well," said Sam, "He is safe, that's for sure. He has the most endearing habit of just putting his hand flat on the middle of my back when I'm upset. I got mad at him at first and shrugged him off because I thought he was trying to tell me to get control of myself and settle down. I'm guessing you know how well that works!

But he said, 'This means that I've got your back; I'm on your side in this. I'll help in whatever way you ask me to.' He's a gentleman.

And he's been good for my art education. Whenever he was home from college, he always asked to see my sketches and encouraged me to try something completely different. He showed me the minimalist work that he does. Many repetitions of tiny objects or shapes. Very pleasing to look at, especially when you back up a few steps.

And later he introduced me to the work of Hokusai, who painted more than a hundred fifty years ago, but he's still the absolute king of woodblock printing. He made the famous

Japanese 'Great Wave.' Marshall and I started out with potato prints at first, because they are way cheaper than wood, and easier to carve."

She fidgeted, rearranging the objects on the table, until Cherie reminded Sam of her eyesight challenges. "You are really going to mess me up if the salt and pepper are not where I expect them to be."

"Sorry," said Sam, moving things back where they were.

Cherie remarked to Sam, "You know, I actually know very little about your life as a teenager and after that. You were so excited to leave. Everyone thought you were coming back before school started. And then you had to get settled out there. To be honest, I was really mad at you for not coming back. And for not being here. We were all set to take Karate that summer. Of course, Bama told me you didn't have a choice, but I was mad anyway."

"That's so weird." answered Sam. "I was furious at you, because you had Bama all to yourself, and I couldn't even call her. No part of it was your fault, but I was mad anyway!"

"Well," said Cherie, "Thankfully, that didn't last too long. Eventually we both grew up a little, I guess, and managed to let it go. That wasn't the world's first feud with no basis in reality! But I'm glad that's behind us."

"So am I," said Sam.

Cherie said, "Someday, I want you to tell me everything about your bus trip cross-country. I want to hear every detail."

"Good grief, Cherie, that was what? 18 years ago!"

"Ok, so just the highlights, then, alright?"

"Sure," Sam agreed, "But there's one more thing I need you to help me think through. I want to have some kind of memorial for Bama. I know you all were at her funeral, but I need this for me."

"Well, not many of her friends actually got to her funeral.

That snowstorm didn't just affect air travel out of Boston, it was pretty bad here, too. People could hardly get out of their dooryards, and the snow just wasn't letting up. Besides all that, some of her best friends were still in Florida. I'm sure that doing something now would be just what we all need! What were you thinking of?"

"Nothing formal," said Sam, as she got up to leave. "But you know how Bama loved a picnic! Maybe a potluck, cook-out, BBQ...a picnic, right on the front lawn."

"I'll tell you what, Sam! Why don't you let me plan this whole thing for you. Between Diana and me, we know everybody who knew Bama. We'll make the calls and make it happen. We'll get the men to move tables and park cars. We'll let you know what's going on as plans progress."

"Thanks, Cherie. If you think Diana will help, that will take it off my plate, and," she said, pulling her note paper from her jeans pocket, "I can concentrate on implementing my very complicated plan to organize things. You are a life-saver!"

When Sam got back to the house, she looked again at Marshall's text. He had been praying for her, and "longed to see her"!

She thought to herself, *Well fine, Mr. Smarty Pants, you sent me a cryptic message that I had to research. Well, research this:* She typed, "NatHistEBWhite" and hit SEND.

That referred to a poem by EB White, in a letter to his wife, Katherine. Sam knew that Marshall would have to look it up. But Bama had sent it to her with a promise to always stay connected even though 3000 miles separated them for half of each year. Sam had memorized it;

The spider, dropping down from twig
Unwinds a thread of her devising:
A thin premeditated rig
To use in rising.
And all the journey down through space,
In cool descent and loyal-hearted,
She builds a ladder to the place
From which she started.
Thus I, gone forth, as spiders do,
In spider's web a truth discerning,
Attach one silken strand to you
For my returning.

SAM HEARD the landline ringing in the kitchen. When she answered it, an unfamiliar voice asked hesitantly, "Is this Nancy Sullivan's house?"

"Yes, it is. This is her granddaughter, Samantha."

"Oh, I'm so glad I caught you. This is Millie Harris. I'm one of her friends from church. I'm so sorry for your loss, dear. She loved her life here of course, and we all enjoyed her garlic, but she so looked forward to flying out west to spend the winter with you."

"Thank you," said Sam. "That's what gave me the strength to breathe...knowing that she was coming out as soon as the garlic was planted in the fall. I had her for the holidays, and she and our landlady became the closest of friends. And, of course, my mother didn't care, as long as Bama was in Mrs. Springer's spare room and not 'interfering' at our place."

"Hmmm, well dear, I never did know your mother. But, well, um, the reason I called is that Nancy and I were trying to get a little free library started here in Royalty. I wonder if I could be so bold to ask if you'd be willing to donate any of her books to the cause?"

"Why, yes, I would. In fact, I've been wondering what in

46

the world to do with them. There are so many, and I just don't have the time or presence of mind for a yard sale. There are a few I'd like to keep, but I'm happy to box up the rest for you. Give me your number and I'll call you when they're ready."

When Sam hung up, she realized that she suddenly had a little more energy. She was beginning to get some ideas about what to do with Bama's clothes, household stuff and quilting things; Cherie and Diana would come through for sure with a nice memorial for Bama; and she had a place to go with all of these books.

From the basement, Sam dragged up the banana boxes she and Anna had claimed from the supermarket, and began tackling the bookshelves.

This wasn't too hard, at all. She decided to only keep books that had sentimental value. Anything she was interested in reading "someday," she made a note of, so she could find it later. Because really, if she loaded the Subaru with all the books she was interested in, the tires would pop.

By late afternoon, Sam had 4 cartons filled for the burgeoning Royalty Free Public Library, and a very small pile in her Things I'm Keeping corner.

She pulled down several dictionaries and reference books and stacked them in another box. But the next dictionary was quite large and heavy. As she set it down into the box, it rattled and a weight inside shifted. *What in the world?*

Sam picked up the book again and inspected it. Inside the cover was a metal lid with a lock.

Oh, great, thought Samantha. *Now where would I find a key?* The book shelves were practically empty by now, so she suspected no key was hidden there. She set the fake dictionary on the kitchen counter until she could locate the means to open it.

Time for tea. While the water was boiling, she poked her

hand into every canister and cookie jar, but no luck. She took the head and shoulders lid off the chicken crock where the garlic for kitchen use was always kept. No key, but no garlic either. Her grandmother must have been depending on other people for quite a while, because as long as Bama was cooking anything, she would never have let that little crock go empty.

Sam took her tea out to the porch to think. Bama was famous for stashing money everywhere. Sam remembered her grandmother sticking her hand into a bathrobe pocket or an old pair of boots and coming up with a twenty dollar bill. Suddenly it occurred to her that the most logical place to find a key would be on an actual key ring!

She hurried back inside. Bama's house keys were on the end table in the living room, right where Samantha had tossed them the first night she was here.

Sure enough, on that ring was a small, double-sided key.

Sam stuck it in the locked 'dictionary' and opened up the hidden safe. Inside was a thick stack of bills in a rubber band, a little box with a diamond ring and wedding band, and a note card. On the note card was printed "Don't forget the moving statues."

She figured the rings were the ones Bama had worn until her knuckles were too swollen to wear them anymore. The moving statues perplexed her; she'd have to ponder that.

And the stack of bills? $893

Samantha suddenly broke out laughing. When Bama collected the money from the farmstand, she'd say, "Well, I'd better go put this in the book." Sam always thought she was talking about record-keeping. Maybe so. But probably what she'd been doing all along was stashing it...in the book! Hopefully, she'd paid taxes on it, but who knew?

In any case, here was motel and gas money for the trip back to California. Thank you, Bama.

That night, Sam had trouble getting to sleep, finally drifting off with blurry half-awake dreams of snatches of this and that, smiling garlic bulbs, students with other-worldly sparkling eyes, and column after column of Statues of Liberty marching in a parade.

"WHAT ARE these big ones called, Bama?"

"That's a Morgan Dollar."

"That's a dollar?"

"Yep. But it's not a dollar to spend, because it's worth a lot more than that."

"How can a dollar be worth more than a dollar?"

"Because of what it's made of, how old it is, and what condition it's in. Here, this one is a Kennedy Half Dollar."

"Weird. It doesn't look like half."

"It doesn't mean the shape. It means it's worth 50 cents."

"Except you're going to tell me it's worth way more than 50 cents, because yadda, yadda ya."

"Right."

"Well, what are these ones called?"

"That's a Walking Liberty."

"Liberty, like the Statue of Liberty? A statue doesn't walk! It just stands there."

"Right you are," said Bama. "The actual word 'statue' means something that doesn't move. So, we have to use our imagination." Bama came over and sat next to Sam on the floor.

"Here look at this, but don't try to get it out of the little case. It's extremely valuable. This one coin could put you through college someday. It's called a Seated Liberty. And it was made 40 years before there even was a Statue of Liberty. It's just the idea of liberty, of freedom. The artist imagined it as a woman."

"Weird"

"Well, look at the coin. If you must think of it as a statue, and not an idea, then that statue is sitting; this one is walking. So yes, I suppose they are moving statues."

SAM SAT bolt upright in bed.

She flipped on some lights and stumbled into the dining room, which had not been used for dining ever, at least not that Sam could remember. It was Bama's sewing room, where she made her quilts. There were two boxes under the table. One was full of folded fabric. The one underneath had some holes on the side, and through them you could see that it was full of fabric too. But inside the fabric was the metal file box full of Grampy's coin collection.

Thank you, Grampy and Bama! And thank you, God, for that dream. I might have given that file box away to a charity shop. Sam remembered that several times Bama had sold some coins and sent her money to help with college expenses... but the 1846 Seated Liberty was still here. It was pretty worn, so maybe it wasn't worth as much as Bama had thought, but Sam decided to treat this coin collection like a retirement account.

The next day, Sam called Diana. "Do you want any of Bama's clothes?" she asked.

"Oh no, dear, I'm way too short and round to fit any of Nancy's clothes."

"Well, there's a brand-new winter coat from Bean's. The tags are still on it. And also, can you use her sewing machine?

"The Bernina? Oh my, I wish! Sadly, I don't sew at all anymore. My hands just don't work very well. But, you know, there is a single mother in our church, Katie Hackett, who's started a mending and alterations shop, down in Damariscotta. I bet she would love to use that machine!"

"Great," said Sam. "If she has a business, I'll just let her have the contents of Bama's sewing room. Anything she doesn't want she can pass along or give to a charity thrift shop."

"You know, that's a great idea. She will really appreciate it; she's trying so hard" said Diana. "I'll send Ted over tonight to load the stuff for you. And why don't you put that coat in the pile as well? Katie is almost as tall as Nancy was. She would probably wear it."

Sam hung up and added some things to her now expanded plan. A plan that was beginning to feel like it just might work.

CHAPTER FOUR

*S*am was back over at Cherie's house, sitting at the kitchen table once again with tea and cookies between them.

"I'm sure I've gained weight this past month or so," said Cherie. "We're getting to be a couple of old ladies...look at us, with our tea and crumpets."

"I don't know what a crumpet is," admitted Sam. "Do you?"

"No, but I'd probably eat it."

"Me too. I think I'd better get back to the city before I get too used to this life. I figure I have a couple weeks. School starts August 12, for teachers. So, I should leave the day after the picnic. How are the plans coming?"

Cherie perked up. "Oh great! It's starting to come together. People are really glad to get a chance to meet you and tell you what Bama meant to them. Some of them are people who knew you as a child, but many are people she met, once she got involved in the local church. Do you happen to know how she got interested in God in the first place?"

Sam smiled, "Well that's part of the larger story I promised you. And it's long after the bus trip. Do you have time for the whole story right now?"

"Yes, as a matter of fact, I do. And you can talk freely; Anna just left with some friends to go roller skating."

"OK then," said Sam. "Here goes. The whole truth and nothing but."

"Our ticket was a one-time special summer deal for one adult and one child, 12 and under. It allowed us to get on and off any one of their buses going anywhere for one month. Mom was in a great mood when we first set out on our road trip. We spent the first couple hours chatting about the plans we had made the other night and all the sights we wanted to see.

I wanted to see the Statue of Liberty. I did get to see it, for thirty seconds from a distance. Mom wasn't too interested in history or landmarks. Her number one was The Grand Ole Opry. My number one was the Georgia O'Keefe Museum and Studio. But there were lots of other things, like The Boston Aquarium. I'll never forget the jellyfish. They are so magical and ghost-like.

I wanted to see the Mile High Swinging Bridge in North Carolina, but Mom said she wasn't ever going back to North Carolina.

My mother had a voucher for a river cruise. It was a steamer, the Louisville Queen, that left from St Louis. She said she bought the ticket cheap from an inmate who'd won it in a poker game. But that woman wasn't ever getting out of prison, so she couldn't use it.

The cruise was really fun, with dinner, and a live jazz band, and the weather was perfect. When we got on the boat, they took our picture in front of the great big paddlewheel and the sign: "Louisville Queen." Then when we disembarked, they handed us our 5x7 photo, made into a postcard. We sent that home to Bama."

Cherie interrupted. "I remember when that card arrived. Bama was very excited for you. But then, when no others came for weeks, she was really worried."

"Yeah. So I found out later." Sam said. "Mom had saved plenty of money, so we were staying in a great hotel, and using a taxi to get around. There was a transportation museum which had covered wagons, buggies, and really old trains.

But then we headed over to Nashville, which took the whole day. I can't remember why, but Mom could not get into the Grand Ole Opry. Either their shows were sold out months ahead, or the building was being worked on, I don't know, but basically Mom's mood went south.

We learned pretty early in the trip that in spite of the advertising on our ticket, the buses don't go anywhere near 'all the great sights' all over this great country. They go to bus stations. We weren't going to get to "see America", we were going to see American bus stations. And they are all alike, with disgusting bathrooms, and maybe a vending machine if you're lucky. I ate more chips and candy on that trip than I had eaten, probably ever!

We always seemed to be plunked down in the center of a city, late at night, with no bus going out till the next day. Sometimes there was a cheap motel within walking distance of the bus station. We had learned that the cheap motels always had free breakfast, as well as muffins and fruit you could stow for later. That one fancy hotel we had in St Louis had a breakfast buffet, but they charged you $12.00 apiece.

We spent hours, sometimes the whole night, in plastic chairs in a station, but often, depending on where we were, the bus station actually closed and locked up for the night. So, we'd have to walk or get a taxi somewhere.

When we got into a motel, Mom would say something like, 'Well, you can watch TV if you want; I can't stand being cooped up like this. I'm going out to find someplace to dance. I need the fresh air and exercise.'

Of course, the next day, she didn't want to get out of bed, so we'd end up staying another night.

Sometimes, we'd find something interesting to do that afternoon, depending on where we were, but I don't remember much. We eventually learned to ask some questions about the destination before we got on a bus, like whether the station was open all night, and whether the neighborhood was dangerous. Once in a while, we found a grocery store, so we'd get yogurt and sandwich stuff, and I'd drink a whole quart of milk at once! We walked a lot, dragging suitcases, to get to a diner or a motel.

Somewhere in the middle of the country, I have no idea where, I remember being in the seat by the window. Another bus, another scratchy seat, another field or factory whizzing by. I turned to her and asked, 'Mom, will you tell me why you left Maine in the first place?'

She just said, 'I was so mad at Bama, I had to get out of there.'"

AT CHERIE'S KITCHEN TABLE, Sam stared off into the distance and thought of that conversation; the things her mother said, hard things that hurt her heart, and that she wasn't going to share with Cherie.

———

"OH. I just had to get out of there. My mother and I did not get along at all. I was so mad at her."

"Why were you mad at Bama?"

"I know you can't see it," she said, "because you had a different life with her than I had."

Mom's face and voice suddenly got really hard. " I knew she had made my dad kill himself."

I just about bounced off the bus seat! "What? He didn't kill himself! Bama told me the police said it was an accident! She said they could see he had tripped on a root and he fell with his gun."

"Well, yeah, that's what they said. They just said that so she could get the insurance money, and pay off the house."

I was stunned by this news. "The police lied?" I didn't know it at the time, but as I got to know my mom more, I realized it was far more likely that SHE had lied. But perhaps she really believed it. It would account for the way she felt about Bama.

My mother went on with her story, "I heard my dad the night before. I heard him say, 'I'm done, Nancy. I can't take it anymore. I've been hanging on for your sake. But no more. I'm going to take care of it, first chance I get.'

"The next morning, he was dead. When I told my mother what I heard, she said he was talking about the itchy, irritated red spot on the side of his face. She had been treating it with herbs and natural stuff, but he'd finally had enough of that and decided to go see a doctor."

Mom was serious. "I might have believed her except that morning before daylight, he was putting on his boots in the kitchen. He was going hunting up behind the house. I'd gotten up to pee. When I passed him on my way back to bed, he said, 'Michelle, no matter what happens, remember that I love you.'

"He always called me Shelly. No one else does. And he often would say stuff like, 'Love you, Shelly baby.' But that morning he said 'Michelle', and he said 'No matter what happens.' That's different, because that morning WAS different. That's what you say when something bad is going to happen."

I wanted Mom's story to stop so I could think about all this.

Besides, other people on the bus could hear her and kept glancing over at us. It was embarrassing.

I closed my eyes and leaned against the bus window. My little finger was tapping up a storm against my leg. But the major storm was in my gut. I had to run back to the stinky little bathroom at the back of the bus.

When I got back to my seat, Mom was still on a roll. "You know, when I get an idea in my head," she told me, "It'll stay there and grow and grow until I have to do something about it."

Mom told me that all through high school, she got more and more angry with her mother, until at last the idea of leaving was too big to ignore. A few months before graduation, she had a chance to leave and she took it.

My mother poked me in the ribs. "Keep your hands still for cryin' out loud. You make me crazy doing that. You're worse than my mother! Sit on your hands and go to sleep. We won't be anywhere for hours."

I sat on my hands, but only my hands went to sleep.

SAM HAD BEEN THINKING about all this, but not sharing it out loud with Cherie. The whole suicide theory felt too personal. So now she continued her story for Cherie.

"So, my mom took off, and gave birth to me, then she left me at Bama's, took off again and had that accident. She got her GED in prison in Raleigh, and the whole time, she thought about what she would do when she got out.

By the time that finally happened, she had taken an HVAC course and knew enough about heating and air-conditioning to get a job as part of their transitional release program. She didn't really like working there. Some of the men were afraid of her because of where she'd been. The rest all hit on her constantly; figuring she hadn't been around a man for so long, she must be an easy mark.

She told me she'd been planning our road trip for years."

Samantha stretched and shook her head a little.

"Those were some of the more somber moments I remember about the trip. But let me tell you about the good parts. The best was New Mexico. Between my piggy bank and the $50 spending money that Bama gave me, I had $89 pinned into my jeans pocket. I was saving that for Georgia O'Keeffe.

Mom tormented me about that money. 'What do you mean you're saving it for her? I'm sure she doesn't need your money.'

'Course not, mom,' I told her. 'She's dead. But I want to make sure I see her museum. My teacher told me once that he even took a tour of her ranch and studio. And that's out in the desert somewhere. Probably not near the bus station.'

Nowhere near, as it turned out.

Our bus didn't even go to Santa Fe. It only went to Albuquerque. We had to pay for a different kind of bus to Santa Fe. But once we got there, the O'Keeffe museum and about five other ones were all within walking distance of the motels and cafés and restaurants. There was even a rattlesnake museum...well, that may have been in Albuquerque, but it didn't matter, because mom absolutely refused. She wouldn't even look at a picture of a snake.

My mother and I finally discovered something we both loved...New Mexican food! And it was everywhere. We tried every little café and taco stand we passed. I think my mother actually had fun in Santa Fe, and we made some good memories.

I'd love to go back there. They have turned an old rail yard into a really cool performing arts space; the stuff I've seen them do on the internet is wonderful.

Well, we got into the museum and used my stash to buy a pewter bracelet with 'Take Time to See' engraved on it, and 'Georgia O'Keeffe' on the inside. I still wear that sometimes. I also bought a sketchbook with her Black Door With Snow painting on the cover, a paperback about her life, and a Ghost Ranch cookbook for Bama.

When we finally got to Los Angeles, mom was not impressed with California at all, and neither was I. I was so tired of riding, and the adventure of something new and different every day had worn off. I knew that the Giant Redwoods were way up north, but I didn't even care by then. I tried not to think about the long bus ride home!

Well, anyway, the neighborhood around the LA bus station was really depressing.

Mom went up to the ticket counter to ask where we could find a motel. When she came back to where I was waiting, she told me, 'The lady said we should wait right here until this other bus comes. It isn't included on our ticket, but it isn't expensive and it will get us a little farther north, where it's safer. She says her daughter lives in North Hills, and it'll be a good place for you.'

That's how we ended up in North Hills at a Stop Inn Motel. Perhaps this was a better neighborhood, but the motel was just as dingy as all the others. The 'art' on the walls was great big colored circles. Modern art, I guess.

We checked in too late for their breakfast buffet, but I still had an apple in my backpack, so I munched on that and turned on the TV. Mayberry reruns again.

Mom said she had paid for two nights at the motel, but she was out of money. I had $4.71 left, which I gave her to go find some groceries.

She took the money and left.

I turned off the TV and dug out my brand-new sketch-

book. I sat on the bed and drew a picture of the door my
mother just walked out of.

I was busy sketching the bathroom door when Mom
burst into the motel room announcing that she got a job!

I just stared at her.

'Didn't you hear me? I got a job…and I met a woman who
offered us her garage apartment FREE for the first month
because she's waiting for the appliances to be delivered!'

'Mom, we have to get back to Maine before school starts.
How can you have a job?'

'Don't be stupid! You want to go back to another winter
in frozen NoWhereVille? We're in sunny California. Enjoy
yourself.'

'Bama's in Maine, and Cherie and my other friends are
there, my school is there, and I'm missing karate with
Cherie.'

'First of all,' said my mother, towering over me and
counting on her fingers. 'You don't take karate, it's just something you want to do. You can start it here. Second: there are
schools here and you don't have to get there in a snowstorm.
There are friends here too. And as for Bama, don't kid yourself: She doesn't want you there. Nobody really wants a kid
around!'

I threw myself on the bed and cried into the pillow. My
gut was killing me, but Mom did not let up. 'So let me get
this through your thick skull right now, young lady. I'm your
mother and you are staying here with me.'

So we stayed. Mom's new job was at the front desk at
CutMax, a salon that had 15 chairs. Even though we had zero
money, my mother always looked like a million bucks! The
manager told her she would fit right into their salon. She was
supposed to answer the phone, put towels and stuff into the
washer and dryer, sweep up, and start tomorrow. But Mom
thought they really hired her because they were amazed that

a skinny white girl was so good at braiding. She told me later that that was part of her 'college education' in prison. CutMax let her show off her cornrow skills on a customer, then said part of her duties would be 'adornments.'

Mrs. Springer had been having her hair cut in the first chair, and when the manager asked Mom for her contact information, she overheard Mom saying we had just arrived in California, and were at the Stop Inn Motel on Santiago Blvd. She's the one who had a garage apartment that we could move into immediately. She wasn't going to charge any rent the first month because it only had an old refrigerator that made noises like a helicopter, a coffee pot and a microwave. They had had to special order a super narrow stove and refrigerator, and they were still waiting for them.

Mom had asked about the rent after the first month, and Mrs. Springer said that when it was ready, she would have it inspected for Section 8 housing, so it would be affordable.

We walked over to see the place. It wasn't an apartment over a garage. It was a little house that used to be a garage. They called it a guest house.

The driveway that went between the guest house and the main house was covered over so it was shady. They didn't use that driveway for cars. It was used like a porch or a patio with chairs, tables and a rug that was made out of straw or plastic or something.

Inside there was a tiny bathroom with a pleated fabric folding door held closed by a magnet. It had a little strip of kitchen along the back wall, with a two-seater booth that must have come from a restaurant. There was a single bed and a sofa. I imagined I'd be sleeping on that sofa till I was an old lady shriveled up from too many years in Sunny California.

Thankfully, Mark and Sharon Springer turned out to be really great. He was retired from the city transportation department, and she used to be a court clerk. And she was so cute. She had a perfectly round face, gray curls about two inches long, and while she wasn't really fat, she sure had a lot of cushion. Definitely huggable.

Even Mom agreed. 'Yep, she's huggable, not like my boney old mother.' But come to think of it, I never actually saw her hug either one of them.

Those first days, while mom was working, I sat outside in the shade and sketched or daydreamed. Sounds pretty peaceful, but inside I was furious! And hopeless. I had been tricked into coming to California, which of course was my mother's plan all along. We had no phone so I couldn't call Bama. And no TV, which was probably good, because a person can only watch so much Gilligan's Island until you go crazy. So, at least this was better than a motel room, mostly because it was free, and way better than sleeping on a moving bus.

One morning I took a chance and reminded Mom that we still had time to get back to Maine before school started.

'Don't be so crazy,' Mom screamed at me. 'I'm not going back to Maine! Ever! Why would I want to? You only want to go back because it's what you're used to. But as soon as school starts, you'll make friends and get involved in life here… and you'll want to stay too.'

'Well, YOU stay here,' I yelled, 'Let me go back. I want to live with Bama!'

'They won't let you use that ticket by yourself. You're a kid. I'm your mother. You're staying here. Besides, if you leave, you'll be responsible for putting me out on the street. Do you want that on your conscience?'

'What are you talking about?'

Mom informed me that she had done all the research while she was in prison. The state of California would pay for most of our rent, we'd have food stamps and health care: but that's only because I was living with her. Without a kid, they give her nothing and there's no way she could earn enough money to live there.

'Without you,' she told me, 'I might as well rot in my mother's attic with all of her other junk! That's what she thinks of me, anyway! Junk!'

After that, she went to work, and I spent a while crying and kicking the side of the sofa. Of course, Mom's information made sense according to what I was finding out about her.

I had been wondering; if nobody really wanted a kid around, what did my mother want me for? And there it was. I was here so mom could get stuff from the state of California. I had wanted to get to know my mother on this trip, and I guess I was doing just that!"

Sam remembered what had happened after her mother left for work that day; what led up to Sam's eventual reunion with Bama.

I WENT OUTSIDE. It was pretty hot in our guesthouse. Mr. Springer had someone coming later to help him fix our air conditioner. At least out here there was a little breeze..

Mrs. Springer came out and sat down across from me. "I don't know how long I can stay out here. This heat is a killer"

"Mrs. Springer," I asked. "How come you're letting us stay here?"

"Oh, honey bear, sometimes the Lord just gives me a kick in the pants! Do you know what I mean? As soon as I heard your mom was new in town and had a daughter, my heart started beating like crazy. I knew I had to invite you two in before my chest exploded. Do you know what I mean?"

"No, not really. Is it like a guilty conscience?'

"Sort of," she said. "Like if you know you should apologize to someone and you feel miserable until you do."

I asked her if she had heart problems. But she assured me she had a perfectly healthy heart. "When the Holy Spirit makes my heart pound, it feels different than if I were running around the block. I can't really explain it very well. Besides, you aren't the first ones to live here. Twice before, this happened with women I met through the court where I used to work.

"We can talk more about that later, but right now, if you don't mind, I'd really love to see what you're drawing."

I handed it over to her. She studied my sketchbook for a while and then handed it back.

"Interesting. It's all doors. And they are all closed."

"Yep!" I answered. "I'm going to use this whole sketchbook for doors."

"Open doors are inviting," Mrs. Springer said. "Why don't you try one of those?"

Suddenly I exploded. Mrs. Springer jumped; I even surprised myself.

"My whole life is closed!" I yelled. "She tricked me into coming here, I hate it and I'm too scared to just leave by myself, and I miss my Bama, and I want to go back to Maine. Nothing here feels like home. Nothing feels safe. Nothing feels right." But I wasn't yelling anymore; I was sobbing and Mrs. Springer had her arms around me.

"Things can get better, if you give it some time."

I shook my head. "I don't see how. I might as well just die!"

Mrs. Springer took my hand and pulled me up out of the lawn chair. "Come into my kitchen, honey bear. It's cool in there and I've got some raspberry lemonade."

The air conditioning felt great and so did the lemonade and banana bread. My life looked better already. And her red and white kitchen was so pretty. Right inside the back door was a long countertop. The bar stools had padded seats and backs. I scooted up into *one of those seats and got comfortable. I didn't know it then, but I would put in a ton of hours over the next ten years doing homework here in this very spot.*

We talked for a while and I told her about the Georgia O'Keeffe museum, and the endless bus trip. I asked if she had any kids, and she told me about their son, who died when he was seven.

I asked to see a picture of him and she went and got one in a frame from the living room to show me. "He was 5 in this picture," she said. "He was laughing at something the dog was doing, and the picture caught his personality just right."

"He looks really sweet. Are you still terribly sad?" I asked her.

"Yes, sometimes," she answered. "But it's been a lot of years and most of the time, I can remember him fondly and thank God we had him as long as we did. We knew when he was born that he probably wouldn't live to be a grown-up."

"Why did he die?" I asked.

"He had CF, Cystic Fibrosis. It's genetic, which means you're born with it. It makes it really difficult for a person to breathe. Back then it was different, but these days, CF people can live much longer, though I imagine they'd have to leave Southern California, because the air pollution would make it worse."

"They should move to Maine," I said. "We don't have air pollution."

"Right," said Mrs. Springer, picking up the phone. "And speaking of Maine, why don't we call your grandmother?"

"Can we? Long distance is expensive. I don't have any money."

"This is important; we won't worry about the cost of long distance."

I told her our number in Maine, she dialed, and handed the phone to me.

As soon as I heard my grandmother's voice, I burst into tears. It took me about ten minutes to get out the whole story.

"Bama, did you know she was kidnapping me? Mom said you knew and you don't want me anyway."

"No, of course I didn't know. And of course, I want you. Always and forever. But I'm not surprised she said that. Nothing about Michelle surprises me. And, it certainly was mean and deceitful, but it's not kidnapping. Unfortunately, she does have the legal right to move you anywhere she wants. Where is she right now?"

"She's at work. I'm over at our landlady's house, Mrs. Springer. She said not to worry about long distance, 'cause this was important.'"

"Well, it is important. I'm so glad you called. I was wondering where you were; I've been worried because I haven't heard a word since I got your photo postcard from the river boat."

"But I wrote you lots of letters. Mom said she mailed them."

"Well, I never got them," said Bama. "Hey, do you think I could talk to Mrs. Springer, please."

Mrs. Springer took the phone into the living room while I poured some more lemonade and spread cream cheese on another slice of banana bread.

After a while, she came back into the kitchen and handed me the phone.

"Hey, I have an idea, Sammi," said Bama. "How's this: as soon as I get the garlic into the ground this fall, I'll fly out to California. Mrs. Springer invited me to stay in their spare room. I'll be there for the holidays and I'll stay until it's time to plant the other stuff in the spring."

"Oh, Bama!" I shrieked.

"Now, hold on a minute," said Bama. "I'll do that, only if you'll promise to stay put and not try to get back here on your own. You also have to start school there with a good attitude, and try to get along with your mother. "I know there's some good in this mess somewhere; I want you to look for it."

"Boys oh boys!" I said, "Will she ever have a fit about you being here!"

"Oh, I'll stay out of her way. Most days she'll never see me. Now do we have a deal?"

66

"Deal!" I shouted. I jumped off the bar stool and ran in a circle around the kitchen. "Yes, it's a deal, Bama! I was thinking I'd never see you again. Wait till you see my new sketchbook. It'll have doors on every page by then. No pond lilies!

"I'm not going to say anything to Mom about you coming. I don't want her to have a meltdown all over me. I'm going to write you a long letter all about the Georgia O'Keeffe museum. And I'll mail it myself."

CHAPTER FIVE

"*Mom, the school is just a couple blocks away. Can we go check it out? I don't even know when the first day is. I won't be so nervous if I know what to expect.*"

"*Yeah, sure we can go sometime next week.*"

"*OK. I'm going to need some clothes, too.*"

"*I'm not made of money,*" *Mom said.*

"*Mrs. Springer says her church has a second-hand store. Could we try there, at least? My jeans are too small. And...*"

"*Second-hand? You want to go to school looking like a bum?*"

"*Mom, why don't we just take a look. Those clothes can't look any worse than the ones I'm wearing. Or maybe I'll just save my money and buy my own clothes.*"

Mom was suddenly very suspicious. "*Save what money?*"

"*Mr. Springer hired me to do his yard work. He's paying me $5.00 every Saturday.*"

"*Five dollars!*" *Mom shouted.* "*Hoo boy! He can spot a sucker when he sees one. I hear those ladies talk at work and I know gardeners are expensive. He got you pretty cheap!*"

"*Well, I'm just a kid, and I'm just helping him, 'cause I can't do the really heavy stuff. Besides, Mr. Springer is going to put...*"

(I stopped myself. I almost let it out that Mr. Springer is putting $30 a week into a savings account so I can go to college. That's a secret. Mom would screech and demand that money if she knew.)

So, I started again. "He's going to put a lot of that junk away in the shed and pull that pile of boards away from the bushes, so I can trim them."

"What makes you think you know how to trim bushes?"

"Mom, I spent every day since I could walk, helping Bama in her gardens. I know how to do a lot of stuff."

"OK, OK. We'll figure something out. But now I've got to get a shower. Paul is picking me up at 7."

SAM GAVE Cherie a generalized summary of Mrs. Springer's lightning fast decision to let them live in the guest house, and why Bama started spending winters in California. Then she went on.

"But apparently Mrs. Springer wasn't the only one that got a kick in the pants from God. Because one day Mr. Springer showed up at our door with a tool bag. He didn't say much, he just measured stuff and left.

He ended up building me a bunk with bookshelves, and underneath where a bottom bunk would be, he made a desk and shelves and a padded corner with a reading light. On the outside, at the foot, was the ladder, a tiny closet that held a half dozen hangers and four big drawers. The best part was a curtain that pulled around the whole thing. I had my own private space.

Mr. Springer insisted it was just home improvement. He had meant to build a bunk in here for years and was just now getting around to it.

When school started, I kept my promise to Bama and reminded myself to have a good attitude every day. And it was really ok, because I generally liked school, and after the first week, I fell into the routine.

Sometime just before Halloween, the school guidance counselor stopped me in the hall and pulled me into her office. I didn't know what was going on. But she was smiling, so maybe it wasn't bad.

'I have a favor to ask of you,' she started. 'Tomorrow morning we'll be having a new student who is actually new in this country. She's really scared and I'd like you to be her friend and help her get used to things.'

'OK, but why me? I'm sort of new myself.'

'I know! That's why I think you two would be a good match. Plus, she doesn't speak much English; she's from Mexico.'

'There are lots of kids here that speak Spanish. Wouldn't they be…?'

'Just the opposite, in fact. If she hangs out with Spanish-speaking kids, that's all she'll hear. Her parents really want her to speak English properly. Her name is America. America Zuneda.'

And so, she and I were assigned to each other, and we did become friends. She was really pretty with the curliest shiny black hair I'd ever seen! She wanted to be called Erica at school, because it sounded more American. We thought it was hilarious that the name America did not sound American! But really, at first she couldn't even say Erica. It sounded like Edica.

We had a Halloween party and a costume parade at school. Erica and I went as a Twix bar. Her mother sewed us a costume that we both fit into. It was great fun. We had to practice walking like a three-legged race, or we got tangled up and fell.

California was definitely cooler as fall progressed, but still warmer even than summers in Maine.

I'd had the date November 3rd circled in red on my calendar for months! Mrs. Springer and I had spent days getting her guest room ready for Bama. She was flying into Los Angeles and taking the airport bus to Van Nuys, which was really close to us.

Finally the day arrived and the Springers and I went to pick her up. I could not stand still, waiting for other people to disembark. As soon as she stepped off the bus I melted into her arms and stayed right there, breathing in her scent, my tears making the front of her blouse wet.

When I finally let her go, Mrs. Springer gave her a hug and said how glad she was to meet her. Bama reached out to shake Mr. Springer's hand, but he said, 'Oh, give me a hug! We're going to be great friends, I just know it.' He was older than his wife, but still pretty strong and rugged. He gave Bama a great big squeeze until she squealed!"

AROUND CHRISTMAS TIME, Erica's church was having a grandparents' luncheon, and of course her own grandparents were still in Mexico, so she invited Bama and me.

After the meal as we were walking out through the hall, Bama stopped at a really colorful poster that was written in Spanish.

'Your English is getting pretty good,' she said to Erica. 'Can you translate this?'

Erica hesitated and read it over. Then she said, 'All of them who receives Him, them who believes in His name, He give to them el potestad, uh, He give power...'

Erica stopped and took a breath. 'He let, they can to be made into the children of God.'

'How can that be?' asked Bama. 'We are all the children of God already. Are you sure that's what it says?'

'Es la Escritura!' said Erica pointing to the reference at the bottom: 'John 1:12'"

Bama wasn't buying it. Erica grabbed our hands and practically pulled us back down the hall and into the kitchen, where she found the pastor up to his elbows in the dishpan. She rattled something off in Spanish, pointing down the hall where the poster hung, and pointing at us.

The pastor dried his hands, asked someone else to take over, and introduced himself. 'Pastor Carlos Gomez. Erica did actually translate that correctly. It does say that we become the children of God, when we receive Him, and believe in his name. It's John 1:12. You can look it up.'

'But everyone is a child of God, right?' asked Bama.

'That's what people say, but actually, while we are all his creation, and He loves us all, we aren't his children until we receive and believe. The Greek word is translated 'power,' but it also means the right or privilege, or the legal authority. We have to be adopted into his family. 'Receiving and believing' completes the adoption. Let's go to my office, get my Bible and have a look at what else God says.'

When we got settled in the office, the Pastor found another verse. 'This is John chapter 3, verses 16-18, God so loved the world, that he gave his one and only Son, so that whoever believes in him will not perish, but have everlasting life. Because God did not send his Son into the world to condemn the world, but that the world through him might be saved.'

'How does that happen?' asked Bama.

'The first step is just to talk to God. Admit you are a sinner, tell him you're sorry, and thank him for sending Jesus to pay your penalty.'

'That sounds way too easy,' I said.

'Oh no,' said the pastor. 'It's very simple, but it's not easy, by any means. It requires complete humility. Admitting you're a sinner. We're told elsewhere to repent. Which means to turn around and go the other way.'

Bama said, 'I can accept that we're all sinners, but we do lots of good things, too. Doesn't that count?'

The pastor smiled, 'It's not like a scorecard or a balance sheet. And I'm glad of that! We could never do enough good to satisfy God. He's perfect and he demands perfection.'

'That's not fair!' I said, shaking my head. 'Who can be perfect?'

'Nobody,' said Pastor Gomez, 'God knows that we can't measure up, but he loves us, so he sent his perfect son, Jesus, to die, paying the penalty for all my sin and yours and everyone's.'

I was indignant! 'He had to DIE? That was harsh!'

'Yes, it was! Forgiving us cost God a lot! But He really loves us. He really loves you! It is pretty simple, like I said. Just admit you have a huge debt you can't pay, believe that Jesus died to pay it for you, and that he rose from the dead.'

'Rose from the dead. Like Easter Sunday?'

The pastor nodded. 'Exactly. Absolutely vital to God's whole plan.'

Bama asked, 'So, is it God or Jesus?'

'Well,' the pastor answered. 'God is who you want, but the only way to get to him is through Jesus. That's the way God set it up. Jesus is the only access. In fact he called himself the Way; that's John 14:6. He also said he was the Door or the Gate. You'll find that in John 10, but wait.'

Pastor Gomez turned and pulled a Bible off the shelf behind him. He looked through it for a minute, put a book-mark in the place and handed it to Bama. He suggested she read the whole book of John. He thought it would make more sense than all these bits and pieces. He also wrote down the references he'd just mentioned.

On the way out, he told us they had bi-lingual services

Sunday afternoons from 1-4:00. It takes that long because everything has to be said twice.

So that was the beginning of Bama's exploration of the Bible. And, of course, it became my search as well, because I rarely let Bama do anything that didn't include me. And I dragged her into everything I did; my schoolwork, my yard-work, and my art and now this.

She and I went to the bi-lingual service each week. It really was a great way to get used to hearing Spanish. Way better than my *Intro to Spanish* class where I could see the words, but rarely hear them used in a sentence. And Erica came with her family to hear the English.

Win all around, except my mother busted me all the time. 'All afternoon in church? That old woman has lost her mind. When I was a kid, she never gave church a thought.'

"So," said Samantha to Cherie, "When Bama came back to Maine that spring, she visited several churches around here and finally ended up with the Wellers at Mid-Coast Community. That's where she discovered others who believed that going to church and helping other people is not what makes you a Christian. Instead, accepting God's forgiveness, that Christ died to provide, is what makes you want to help others and get together with like-minded people at church."

"I know what you mean," said Cherie. "I was raised in church, but it wasn't till I fell in love with Jesus that I could accept my failing eyesight, and know deep inside somewhere, that I was OK in God's opinion. Bama and I had some good talks about that."

Sam agreed. "I finally got on board, with Bama's help and the help of Erica and the Springers and, well, Marshall, too."

Cherie asked, "Hey, do you want something to drink? I want you to continue your story."

"Yeah, just some water please."

They got settled again and Sam continued.

"Well, let's see. Where was I? Right, well, of course my period started that fall and thankfully, did not start at school. That kind of embarrassment is deadly in seventh grade. But Mom wasn't home. I kind of knew what was going on, but it was scary just the same. And I was not prepared for the pain in my gut. I didn't think that kind of cramp was what the books were talking about.

So, I stuffed some paper towels in my underpants and went over to see Mrs. Springer.

I whispered to her. Mr. Springer was very busy putting silverware away, and didn't look up.

We went into the bathroom and I told her I thought my period had started but that something wasn't right, because it hurt so bad.

She settled me down, gave me some Tylenol and some pads that she used sometimes for bladder leaks, but they were the same thing. She told me to change them often, and that I could go lay down if it helped, but most people don't have to stay in bed. She said it usually lasts several days or as much as a week and then happens every month. I asked her if she meant every month forever.

'Well no,' she said, ' just until you're about 50. Then your body will shut it down.'

'Is it going to hurt this bad every month?' I asked her.

'Probably not, but some people do have painful periods. Give your body a couple months to get used to things. If it's really painful to the point where you can't do your regular day, talk to your mom. She can take you to a doctor for some help.

'But it's really OK to just take it a little easy, and take a pain reliever when you have your period. And, Samantha, this is not something that you are meant to do by yourself. I'm so glad you came over to talk to me. You know, I'll listen to anything, not just about this.'

Then she gave me the talk about how every woman in the history of the world has gone through this; it's the way it's supposed to be. And she told me that once in a while I would get blood on my clothes or sheets; it happens to everyone; just scrub it out with cold water and soap. We talked some more, but later, when I told my mom, she gave me some rather alarming information that Mrs. Springer hadn't mentioned.

'What this means is, now you can get pregnant. So don't be messing around with boys.' I had another talk with Mrs. Springer about that!

By the time I was in 10th grade, I quite often spent the night in the great big king-size bed in Springer's spare room, whether Bama was there or not, 'cause mom had a lot of…'friends over,' shall we say. I tried to avoid them as much as possible. Some of her dates were ok, but a lot of them were pretty creepy.

Samantha paused. "Um, well, this part; I don't usually talk about this. Marshall knows, and of course the Springers were right there. It's terrible, but I want to tell you. OK?"

"Sure," said Cherie. "If it's something you need to tell, I'll listen."

"Well, one of her boyfriends tried to rape me. He didn't succeed."

One day after school, I decided to get my shower right away, and be done before mom got home. I knew she had a dinner date with Ronnie, and would be in a hurry to get ready.

I came out of the shower with my bathrobe on, drying my hair with a towel, when I heard the key in the lock and the door open. I looked up from under the towel and it wasn't mom. It was Ronnie! He shut the door behind him.

Ronnie smiled his sleazy little grin and said, "Michelle gave me her keys and asked me to wait for her here till she got done working." He waggled the keys in the air like a prize.

Alarms were going off in my head. "Wait outside! You shouldn't be here!"

He continued, inching a little closer all the time. "No! It's 100 degrees out there. Besides, it's nice to see you."

I grabbed my robe tighter around me.

Ronnie said, "It looks like you were expecting me, or do you have a boyfriend hiding somewhere?" He stepped closer, put a hand on my shoulder and peered into the bathroom.

I absolutely freaked! I flipped his hand off me and shouted, "Get out! Get! Out!"

Ronnie acted like we were having fun. "Oh, I've always loved a feisty red-head. Ole Ronnie here can show you a good time."

"Get out" I screamed at him."Leave me alone."

But instead of leaving, he pressed himself right up against me. "Don't pretend you don't want this. You've been teasing me ever since I met you."

"I have not! That's just your sick imagination!"

He grabbed me with both hands. I was screaming and struggling; he was gripping my arms so tightly, I could hardly move.

My brief interest in karate did not help me at all, except to make me determined that what Ronnie was trying to do was NOT going to happen.

I screamed even louder. If I couldn't stop him, I could at least burst his eardrums.

I brought my knee up fast and hard, and made contact, just as Mr. Springer crashed through the door.

Ronnie barked a nasty word, leaned to one side and collapsed. Mr. Springer literally picked Ronnie up by his shirt and his belt and threw him out into the breezeway. I wrapped my robe around me and curled up on the bed sobbing.

SAMANTHA SAID TO CHERIE, "Mr. Springer heard the commotion and broke in the door just in time. Mrs. Springer went inside and called Mom, then she called the police. Mom showed up a few minutes later and went ballistic! 'You stole my keys, you slimeball. Bad enough you're cheating on me, but with my own daughter? She's 15, for crying out loud!'

"'Mark, keep him right there.' she told Mr. Springer. 'Don't let him move till the police get here.'

"She found me inside and asked me lots of disturbing questions. That, and all the stuff the police woman asked me, made the whole nightmare even worse."

Sam stopped. And Cherie felt for her hand. "I'm so sorry that happened to you. That's enough detail, but I will listen if there's more you want to say."

Sam said, "Thanks. We were going to have to go to court and testify, but at the last minute, Ronnie pled guilty and they put him in jail. The judge also fined him, ordered state-provided counseling for me, the cost of which was added to the fine, and he even awarded Mr. Springer the cost of fixing our door."

Sam sat staring at the tablecloth for a minute.

"Wow" said Cherie. "That would have done me in!"

"Well, I sure was a hot mess for a while. The counseling helped me settle down a little. At first, I'd go places with a group, but as for being alone with a guy, no way. But that fall, when Bama came out, she gave me a 'talking to.'

She helped me to get mad instead of being afraid. When I was attacked, I did the right things; I fought back and I screamed. And then, I had sweet loving people to rescue me. Thankfully, my mother didn't blame me, or try to minimize Ronnie's responsibility. Bama convinced me I was strong enough not to let one stupid guy destroy my life.

Now, I'm good, even though I've always been pretty cautious about making commitments to people, and who I go out with. After all, I saw my mother fall in love twice a week, and I've been careful not to follow her example."

"Well now," said Sam. "I got myself into a dark place with this story, but there are lots of positive things to tell you. So let me change the subject here."

But Cherie wasn't ready to move on. "Before you do that, Sam, perhaps you might think about whether this is why you are holding Marshall at a safe distance, instead of admitting your true feelings for him."

Sam just shook her head and muttered, "No, no, I don't think so."

After a few seconds of awkward silence, Cherie relented. "Alrighty then, please continue with your story."

"Sure," said Sam. "Ronnie's out of jail, but with lots of restrictions. No one's seen him around for ages and I don't really think about him at all."

"Really?" asked Cherie, "You don't think of him at all? That kind of trauma isn't something a person just forgets."

"Well, I don't mean I've forgotten about it. But it no longer torments me, or invades my dreams."

"Right," said Cherie."Let's go sit in the living room. These kitchen chairs weren't built for a marathon. In your story, you're still a teenager. Tell me about the rest!"

They resettled themselves more comfortably, and Sam picked up her monologue again.

"Well, OK, the short version is: I graduated from high school, turned 18, and my mother took off. The Springers advised me to stay right there in their guest house. They said they would not charge me any rent if I stayed in school, even during summer sessions, and kept the yard work up. So that's what I did. And about a year later Mr. Springer died.

A couple years after that, the Las Vegas police contacted

me, because a Michelle Sullivan had been killed by her boyfriend and they found my senior picture in her wallet. They asked me to go to Vegas and identify her body.

I called Bama and let her cry for a while over the phone. I was so sorry for my grandmother, but really, all I felt was the lead in my gut. I almost flew to Maine right then, but I had to miss classes to go to Las Vegas, and I had to make some sort of burial arrangements. Mrs. Springer helped me, of course, and Bama flew out just for a couple days. The garlic wasn't in the ground yet."

DURING THAT VISIT, Bama finally talked to me about Grampy's hunting accident. We sat in my little guest house and I held her hands gently; the skin on her knuckles was stretched tight, red and shiny. Her arthritis had gotten worse than I remembered.

'Bama, Mom said Grampy committed suicide, and the police lied about it for your sake.'

Bama hung her head and slowly shook it back and forth.
"When Michelle got an idea in her head, there was just no getting rid of it. In spite of what we see on television, the police are not in the habit of defrauding insurance companies. Besides, they took a ton of pictures and the insurance company did their own investigation. It was pretty clear it was an accident.

I lost my husband and my only child on the same day. Michelle was always cantankerous and stand-off-ish, but when her father died, she pulled away from me and I never got her back. And all I had was her physical presence for 17 years. I never got to experience the bond one can have with a child, until there was you!

You were such a gift. You were the one good thing Michelle let me have and I will always be grateful to her and to God for you.

When she took you to California and I didn't hear anything, I grieved all over again. The garlic became my retreat, my life-saver, *and for sure I put a lot of extra time and attention into Cherie, because she was always there. And I knew she missed you as much as I did."*

We had some long talks about whether you'd come back and why you didn't write.

And oh my! The Springers! They were generous and wise enough to realize that you and I needed each other and made a place in their lives for both of us. If you remember, I told you there was some good to be found in that mess. And there certainly was.

"WE COULD NOT FIND anyone who knew my mother in Las Vegas." Sam said to Cherie. "So, in the end, we had my mother cremated, and Pastor Gomez made a little ceremony out of putting her ashes in the flower garden in front of the guest house. Erica's family was there, the Springers and Marshall, as well as a couple of my friends from school. When Bama went back home, she took with her a little brass heart with some of mom's ashes sealed inside. I didn't want one."

Cherie asked gently, "Do you hate her?"

"Oh no," said Sam. "She wasn't evil, or even deliberately mean. She was extremely self-absorbed and I think she was so desperate for someone to love her, but she pushed away anyone who tried, even me. She didn't do relationships of any kind very well. I kind of blame that on all her years in prison. She had been a sad, angry teenager who made some thoughtless, stupid moves that had a huge impact on the rest of her life."

Sam finished up with, "In the end, there certainly was good to be found in my being hauled away to California. Bama and I figured it was the Holy Spirit who prompted Mrs. Springer to have her hair cut just as mom walked in for a job and to offer mom and me a place to live. He had it all set up to welcome me to California. Then she invited Bama, a complete stranger, to come and stay for the winters. That's not something the average person would do. But the Springers were not average!

Over the years, I've become more and more grateful for people who will listen to the little voice in their spirit, and take action.

As for my mom, I do feel grateful that, whatever her motives were, she went through with the pregnancy that produced me, and I wasn't in the car with her when she wrecked it.

I heard a song on an oldies station once that went: 'looking for love in all the wrong places.' That was my mother.

So no, I don't hate her. I was over-the-top angry with her at first, then really disappointed. But little by little, I figured out how to look after myself, and get what I needed from others around me.

So, there. That's my story, and I'm stickin' to it!"

"Wow." said Cherie. "That's a lot to take in. A whole life-time in one afternoon! But I do feel like I know the adult you a little better. Thanks for sharing yourself with me."

"Well," said Sam, "You haven't been in your kitchen making waffles for 18 years. Tell me about you!"

Cherie thought that was pretty funny. "Sometimes it feels like I've been doing nothing but making waffles! For sure, these days, my ADL's as the doctors call them; my activities of daily living, take longer than they would if I were completely sighted.

But right out of high school, I could still see fairly well. I worked in the office for J.P. Crawford. My job was to contract loads to keep their trucks on the road. It was mostly telephone and fax machine, but also a lot on the computer. I could enlarge the type to make things easier. Of course, that's where I met Nelson.

While we were expecting Anna, both my parents died. Dad had had emphysema for years; but then he contracted pneumonia and that was just too much to handle. Mom died about six months later; colon cancer. Neither one lived to see their grandchild.

But my in-laws are over in New Brunswick and we do get together with them every couple months. But other than that, Nelson, Anna and I have been pretty much on our own. That's why we adopted Bama. She's always been my grandmother, no matter what you say!"

Sam laughed at that ancient controversy. They heard the chime from the kitchen clock announce that it was 4:00 pm. "Oh dear," said Cherie. 'I'd better make a start on supper."

Sam agreed, "I'll get back up to the house. Still a ton to do."

As she headed out the door, Cherie called after her. "Oh Sam! It's time for the garlic. How about tomorrow morning early, before it gets too hot."

"Sure," laughed Sam. "It's not going to get too hot for me, but I'll cut you some slack. Meet you out there at 7?"

"7 a.m. it is," said Cherie. "Wear a hat; the deer flies are insane. And remember we're not pulling the garlic."

"I know, I know! You're worse than Bama! We're digging the garlic. See you in the morning."

CHAPTER SIX

Sam spotted Cherie and Anna heading across the field and hurried to catch up with them. The sun was up, but not above the trees just yet. Light filtered through, but most of the garlic was in the shade.

The chickens were out of their run, enjoying a morning of freedom, searching for bugs and berries. Sam thought they were delightful; such busy little things fussing about the field.

"Good morning! I brought coffee." Sam hollered.

"Good morning to you!" answered Cherie.

Sam was still amused by the chickens. "How do you get them back in the pen?"

Anna answered her. "Oh, I just rattle the bag of mealworm treats, and they'll follow me anywhere. We can't leave them out all day. There are too many things in the woods that like to eat chickens."

"Alrighty, let's get busy," said Sam, as they approached the raised beds. "Anna, you're in charge."

"Nope!" said Anna, much to Sam's surprise. "Mom's in charge. I'm the gopher and the runner."

Cherie handed Sam a pair of gloves, a trowel and a burlap sack. "You might want to sit on this to avoid splinters. And turn around a minute so Anna can stick a deer fly trap on the back of your hat.

"Now here's the deal, in case you forgot. I'll work one side, and you work the other. We'll both be able to reach the center by sitting here on the edge of the bed. Brush away the dirt from the stem with your fingers until you can feel the curve of the bulb. Gently push the tool down beside the bulb and under it. Then lift it up. Don't pull on the stem.

Anna lifted a stack of baskets off the wagon and handed one to Sam. She told her it had been custom made for harvesting garlic. It was well balanced and long enough to put the whole plant in, with one end covered.

Cherie continued with her instructions. "Brush the dirt off of the bulb, and put the plant in the basket with the bulb under the covered part. We don't want to shock these little guys with the bright sun. Anna will take the baskets up to the shed as we fill them."

"Got it! Let's do this!" Sam said.

They worked across from each other for nearly an hour, Anna taking their filled baskets and keeping them supplied with empty ones. The twisting and bending put a strain on Sam's back. She had to stop and stretch. She felt around under the folded burlap bag she had been sitting on. "No wonder my butt hurts! I've been sitting on a rock." She pitched it across to Cherie.

Cherie looked up. "Hey, remember when we were going to be geologists? We quit after we realized that practically every rock we found was the same kind."

"Yeah," said Sam. "I think that was right before our movie star/ singer stage."

Cherie flipped a garlic stalk over with the bulb as a

microphone and belted out, "Who is the one you're clinging to, instead of me tonight?"

Sam joined in, "And where are you now, now when I need you?"

She grabbed Cherie's free hand, and they stood up, arms connecting the space between them over the garlic crop. "In the words of a broken heart, it's just emotion, taking me over."

They finished the song in a great exaggerated flourish, as Anna was coming back from the shed.

"What was that noise?" wondered Anna. "I thought someone was killing the chickens."

"Sorry," said Sam, "we were not murdering chickens, but we did a fairly thorough job on Destiny's Child."

Anna stopped in her tracks. "Whose child?"

"You know who Beyonce is. She started out in a group called Destiny's Child."

"Did she wear clothes back then?"

"Yeah," said Sam. And then she thought for a minute. "Well, sort of." She placed another stalk of garlic in her basket.

"Oh, please." begged Cherie. "Let's not get Anna started. As you've noticed, she believes in free expression when it comes to clothes, but she's completely intolerant of people who choose not to wear them. She looks like a kid, but she's really an old fuddy duddy."

Anna sputtered, "I'm not a fuddy duddy and that's a stupid word anyway." She picked up Sam's full basket and put it into the wagon.

"Well," Sam said. "I happen to think we sound pretty good. Let's get a bus and go on the road. Hey, do me a favor, Anna, teach yourself to play the guitar this afternoon? Your mom and I are getting a band together."

Anna let out a dismissive little snort, but Cherie picked

up on Sam's diversion. "What should we call ourselves? How about Garlic Pickers."

"No, I think it should be Bulbs of Backache," suggested Sam, bending over the garlic bed again.

Cherie countered, "That's terrible. Wait, I know! Perfect band name: Galactic Sojourn!"

"Well," Anna announced. "I'm not playing guitar for you two. You guys are nuts." She adjusted her cap and stomped off, back to the shed, with the loaded wagon.

"Fine then," Cherie called after her. "When we make our millions, we're not sharing...just saying."

WHEN THE LAST garlic bulb was out of the ground and in the shed it was nearly mid-day.

Sam brushed off her pants and announced. "OK you two, lunch is on me. Let's go to that little take-out place on Route 1. They have picnic tables outside, so it doesn't matter how we look."

They piled into Bama's Subaru and on the way, talked about the need to call Bama's customers, lamenting the fact that this was the end of an era. No more Royalty Garlic.

Usually, the largest and most perfect bulbs were kept for seed. But they really were gift quality. Sam wondered if they could give one to everyone who came to the funeral/picnic.

"That way," she said, "They can plant them at home and have a little memory growing for themselves."

"Hmmm, I like that idea." mused Cherie. "I guess you've decided to sell the house?"

"Yeah, it pains me, but it's really the only thing to do. I have an appointment with a realtor on Monday."

"What about the chickens?" asked Anna.

Sam shrugged. "I haven't decided yet. I'll let you know if I need some help moving them.

"Hey, maybe we should cook them all in a great big chicken soup to serve at the memorial!" she added, half-jokingly.

"You can't eat Miss Betty," said Anna. "If you do, you'd have to cook Gerald, too, and cat soup would be gross."

They were at the Blue Moose Café and Bakery by then, starving and ready to dig in.

While they were eating burgers and french fries made from freshly cut potatoes, Sam got a text from Marshall: *2jhn12* She didn't share it with Cherie…she'd look it up and then decide.

When she got home, she found the verse in the New Testament. 2nd John 12: "I have much to write to you, but I do not want to use paper and ink. Instead, I hope to visit you and talk with you face to face, so that our joy may be complete."

ON MONDAY MORNING, Sam checked her list and put it in her bag with Bama's will and several copies of the death certificate. Her appointment with the realtor wasn't until 3 pm but she had quite a few errands to complete while she was in Rockland.

Her first stop was at Agway for two extra bags of chicken feed, and a big bag of mealworm treats.

Then she went to Collier's Quick Print. She pulled out her phone and located the picture she had taken that morning of the surface of the lily pond desk. She asked the woman at the counter, "Can we get this photo off my phone and print it poster size, like 16 X 20? Two copies, please.

"Sure thing," said the clerk. "But if I blow it up that big, it'll be a little blurry."

"No problem," said Sam. "It's a painting of fog, so I don't think it will make much difference. I have a quote I want to put on them. I'll do the lettering myself, but I'd like to purchase plastic frames for them."

While she was waiting for her prints, she browsed the store. She found some small muslin bags, and went back to the counter to ask to have them imprinted with her grandmother's full name and the dates that she had lived.

She also found some attractive memorial stickers to put inside the books for the new little library. These she wanted printed with "In loving memory of Nancy Sullivan"

"I'll tell you what," said the clerk. "We close at 5:30. If you can come back around 5, I'll have all this ready for you and packaged up to go. How's that sound?"

"Great!" said Sam. "I'll see you then."

Sam hurried off. She had to visit the County Records Office and the lawyer before her appointment with the realtor. She sent up a prayer for wisdom and clear thinking.

When Samantha first entered White-McDaniel Realty, the shiney empty tables and desks turned her off, like no one actually worked there. But once she met Catherine McDaniel, she realized she was in good hands with these professionals. The woman was smartly dressed, with a no nonsense short haircut, and little make-up. She seemed to understand Sam's plan immediately.

Sam was actually surprised at how easily arrangements could be made. The realtors were coming out to see the house on Wednesday, and they would work together with the lawyer to finalize everything.

By 4:30 they were wrapping up. Catherine stood and shook her hand, "Well, Samantha, it was a pleasure to meet you. See you Wednesday."

Sam picked up her printing, and got in the car, at last feeling settled, trusting that the decisions she'd made were the right ones. Now to get through the memorial picnic. She'd check with Cherie and Diana to see what remained to be done. Saturday was only 5 days away. And she planned on leaving the following morning.

On her way back from town, Sam stopped at Ted and Diana's before she pulled into her own driveway.

"Oh, Hi Cherie! Didn't know you were here!"

"Anna walked me over. Diana asked me to bring my mending. That's one chore that just requires too much concentrated effort. It's exhausting."

"Chore indeed," quipped Diana. "With your bad eyes and my bad hands, it's a hoot! But we do manage to get a button on now and then."

Cherie laughed. "Well, things are looking up! As of this morning, I'm officially on track to see if I can use those new iSight glasses. I have an appointment next month in Portland.

"Glasses?" asked Diana. "What about the dog?"

"I put the dog on hold for now, because the glasses seem less complicated. They're fairly new technology. I don't know how they collect information and get it past my damaged retinas into my brain, but they do. There's no peripheral vision, but they would pick up whatever is directly in front of me. A guide dog can keep me from walking into a manhole, but he won't do my mending! With this headset, I think I could be more independent. I don't have all the information yet.

"Amazing!" mused Diana, as she got up to stop the tea kettle whistle.

"Wow," said Sam. "I bet they cost a bundle!"

"Yes, they do, but there are organizations doing fund-raising and setting up access to grants and financing. And I bet you never thought that a trained dog could cost up to $75,000. Usually, that cost is sponsored by some corporation. But then you have vet bills, you have to feed it, and as Anna observed, "It poops!'"

"For sure," said Sam, "poop is a factor to consider, but having a dog would be so much fun!"

"Well," added Cherie, "It's not a pet. I'd have to go to Boston or New York for weeks of training. I'd have to be paired up with the right dog, and then learn to "use" him. You have to learn to be vigilant and very, very careful. It's well trained, but it is still a dog, and susceptible to the same distractions, diseases and injuries that any other dog is. The glasses seem simpler."

"This is so exciting, Cherie." said Diana, who was still at the stove. "If this works out, it will be a whole new life for you."

"I know, and it will take a lot of the pressure off of Anna, as well.

"Oh, right!" said Sam. "The reason I stopped is to see what else needs to be done for Saturday."

Diana shifted topics with great enthusiasm. "I talked this morning with Rose Embleton. They just got in from Florida. They stayed longer than usual this year 'cause Charlie was having cataract surgery. But they're here now and excited about the memorial."

Cherie added. "So that makes 42 definites and 4 maybes."

"Hmmm," mumbled Sam. She showed them the little garlic gift bags she had just had printed. "Good thing they came in a pack of 50. Hope I don't run out."

"Don't worry Sam, there will be plenty. Most of the couples will just take one. And it's a potluck, so there will be more than enough food. Brenda Henning is doing a sheet cake that will be fabulous as usual. Jean Townsend is bringing a huge vat of her famous Arnold Palmer with a Kick."

"Right," said Diana. "She'll never reveal what provides the kick, but she swears it's not alcohol. I've always suspected it's Dr. Pepper or Moxie but there's not enough of it to really tell. Maybe it's ginger.

"Anyway, Nelson and Ted will get tables from the church and set them up Saturday morning. They'll put some cars in our driveway, some at Cherie's. There's also space behind your shed to park the cars of those who can't walk very well. Expect people to start showing up around 3 pm."

"Oh!" added Diana. "Pastor Hitchcock has declared himself grill master for the day. People are bringing their own meats. So just make sure the propane tank is full; he'll take care of the rest."

Cherie said, "Also, Gordy Ferris is bringing a pan of baked rice from the restaurant, as well as enough condiments for everything and everyone.

Sam looked a little bewildered. "So, what can I do? Maybe plates and stuff?"

"Nope." answered Cherie. "All that is coming with Gordy. And real silverware! He says plastic forks are from the pit of hell. His Dad was such a buddy of your grandfather, he wanted to cater the whole event, but we convinced him that a potluck was more Bama's style, and it would give people a chance to feel part of things."

Diana gave Sam a hug. "There is something you can do. This is a wake for Nancy, but really, a closure party for you. After we eat, everyone will have a chance to share their memories of your grandmother. Then, it will be your turn. People will want to hear from you. So, think about what you want to say. Then we'll turn the music up and have a good time."

. . .

Sam dropped Cherie off at home and when she drove up Bama's driveway her phone dinged with another text from Marshall.

Ps204

Sam looked that up as soon as she got inside. Psalm 20, verse 4; "May he give you the desire of your heart and make all your plans succeed."

"Just right," thought Samantha. "Thank you, Lord! That's confirmation. The plans I made are good ones!"

Sam shot out the reply to Marshall: *All is well. See you soon*

Samantha spent the next few days gathering things into boxes for the auction. The realtor had advised her that the house would bring a better price if it were empty. The household auction was set for Sept. 3, and before she left, her part was to get as much as she could into lots that could be sold together.

She had asked Ted Weller to come look at the tools and unidentifiable things in the shed, to see if there might be something of real value.

"If there's anything here that Bama might have borrowed from you, or anything that's actually yours, please take it back. I wish there was something here that I could give you to remember her by."

"Oh, my goodness, dear," said Ted. "I guess you wouldn't know this, but when your grandfather died, Nancy literally gave me all his guns. Understandably, she didn't want them in the house. And she also threw in his truck in the bargain. You might not remember that old green Ford 150 I had."

"Oh! I DO remember that truck. When we had a snow-storm, Bama and I would sit at the window and wait for that old truck to make its way up the drive. I loved watching you plow."

Mr. Weller laughed. "Well, that was the only new vehicle your grandfather ever bought. Right off the showroom floor. He drove that for the rest of his life.

"By the time Nancy gave it to me, we knew it was ready to give up the ghost. It was too rusty to pass inspection. But, I used it as a plow truck for another 10 years, until the rust was so bad, I couldn't properly attach the plow blade.

"We loved your grandmother, honey. We have lots to remember her by."

LATER THAT EVENING Sam called Cherie to make sure they would all be home. "I want to talk to you guys all together. Anna, too."

"Come right over," said Cherie. "We're all right here watching Jeopardy. We're getting some answers right, but they never give us any money."

Sam loaded up the large landscaper's wagon with a box of garlic, a gallon-size glass jar with Bama's saved seeds, and the garlic baskets. She slung her bag over her shoulder and pulled the wagon across the field and down through the woods path to Cherie's house.

CHAPTER SEVEN

"Ok," she began when they were all settled in Cherie's living room. "I need to make a little speech first." Sam cleared her throat and then continued. "You guys have not just been neighbors, and friends. You are family. Nelson, Cherie, Anna, you treated Bama like she was your own mother. She depended on you for so much. And I wasn't here to help at all."

"Well, we just…" Nelson began, but Sam stopped him.

"Please let me finish." She took a breath, gathered her feelings and thoughts, and then continued.

"Sometime next week, a lawyer from Trask and Gibbons will be contacting you with something to sign. I've already spoken with them. I have deeded the field, the gardens and the henhouse over to Anna, held in trust by you two until she's 21. I'm just selling the house with the lawn, the backyard and flower gardens around it. The part of Bama's property that is behind here; that's yours now."

All three of them just stared at her.

"I'm serious. Anna, the chickens and the garlic beds are yours. You are the only person I would trust with things that

95

were so precious to Bama. And, there's a wagon full of stuff out by your back steps. The pond lily desk is yours, too, Anna. Although I only got it as far as my front porch, if you wouldn't mind picking it up, please, Nelson. It wouldn't fit in the wagon. Oh, and please get the screens from the loft of the shed. You may want them for drying garlic. If there's anything else you want, please take it before the auction.

"In the desk, there are the lists and labels and boxes, and a business plan of Bama's that I found. It's called "Thyme In a Bottle" and it's a plan for making and selling herbal teas and essential oils. You guys may be able to do something with that someday.

"Also," Sam dug around in her bag and produced an envelope, which she handed across the coffee table to Anna. "This is a very small start to an education account. There's just the bare minimum in there now, but if you faithfully put a little bit in each week, it will grow, just like seeds in the garden… and you'll have money for college. Someone did that for me, when they had no obligation to do so. I'm just paying it forward, as they say."

They sat for a moment in silence, then Sam caught Anna's eye, and motioned for her to come over and give her a hug. Anna cried for a minute on Sam's shoulder. Then she gave Sam a great big noisy kiss on the cheek. "You are the best, ever. Thank you. Thank you. Thank you. I'll do my very best, Sam. I promise."

Sam stood up to leave. "And please don't think you have to keep things just the way they are. There are no conditions. Do whatever you want with the property. But you may eventually want to put a fence up to keep the chickens contained in the field. You'll soon have new neighbors, and they may not appreciate a Gerald and Miss Betty showdown waking them up in the morning.

"One more thing, Nelson. The realtor said that the farmstand is not an asset. How hard would it be to move it over to your driveway, unless Anna doesn't want it?

Suddenly Anna appeared between her parents. "The farmstand? Of course, I want it. How else can I sell my eggs? And Dad, we need a refrigerator in there. That old cooler is gross!"

"Yes, ma'am," said Nelson with a little salute. And then, "No problem, Sam. It's hard to see because of the weeds grown up around it, but that little building is on skids. I can just drag it over here with my pick-up. In fact, I'll ask my friend to bring his Bobcat over and scoop out a decent parking space.

They all gave Sam a hug and said goodnight.

THE DAY of the picnic dawned cloudy and drizzly, but by 10 am, the sun was shining brightly. After lunch, tables and chairs started showing up. Sam brought out the flowers she had picked from the backyard gardens, but more flowers arrived with the food; people were milling about, visiting and chatting.

As dishes arrived, Anna arranged them on the table, then rearranged everything all over again when the next dish showed up.

At last, Pastor Hitchcock got folks' attention, blessed the food, thanked God for Nancy's life, then announced, "The grill is hot. If you have meat to cook, bring it up. Whatever I don't eat, I'll give back to you when it's done."

Later, when people started sharing things about their relationship with Nancy Sullivan, Samantha was bowled over.

Bart Landry stood up and said, "Years ago, I lost my job one summer, just after Martha had surgery. With neither of us working, we were having a hard time of it. A bag of vegetables and two dozen eggs appeared on our porch every week until fall, when I finally got hired at UPS. Nancy thought she was being sneaky, so we didn't let her know we saw her dropping them off."

A woman Sam hadn't met said she worked at the Women's Recovery House. Everyone who graduated from the program went home with a brand new quilt made by Nancy Sulllivan. Last count, they'd given away 37 and they still had a closet full.

A young man stood and introduced himself, "I'm Bruce Varney. I manage the homeless shelter. Some of you know that Nancy and Diana folded our laundry every Monday for years. That was a necessary chore, of course, and much appreciated. What you may not know is that folding laundry was just an excuse for Nancy to be there and love on people. We have had some volunteers that we had to let go, because they were haughty and insulting to our residents. But Nancy loved those women, encouraged them and most of all, respected them all, men and women alike. We are thankful that we still have Diana, but, for sure, Nancy will be hard to replace.

Stories like those went on for half an hour. Sam had expected to hear nice things; one does at a funeral. And she had always thought her Bama was extraordinary, but as the afternoon wore on, she realized that others felt the same way.

Finally, it seemed things were wearing down, and Sam stood up.

"Is there anyone else who wants to say something, before I say a few words?"

A voice from back under the maple tree called out. "I would, if you don't mind."

It was a small, dark-skinned woman with a ponytail full

of braids that hung to her waist. No one seemed to know her and Sam had not seen her arrive.

"My name is Libby Hannaford. I'm too embarrassed to tell you the circumstances I was in when I first met Nancy, so let me just say that she found me in those circumstances and she literally rescued me. She put herself in danger to save me from harm; I was very suspicious of her, but she fed me for months and helped and encouraged me in tons of ways. She let me stay here, up in her little upstairs room. I stayed in the house or the backyard, because I didn't want anyone to know where I was.

"Once, she said something about Jesus, and I spit all over her and her faith. But she continued to help me. When I got on my feet, I managed to insult her, questioning her motives, and I took off for Massachusetts. I never contacted her again. I at last came to my senses, and by the time I finally thought I had the courage to apologize to her, I found out she had died.

"So that's why I'm here; to apologize to you all.

"There is a poem called "ANYWAY" that's usually attributed to Mother Teresa…you're probably familiar with it, so I won't try to quote it. But it is a picture of Nancy Sullivan. My version of it is this:

"I took advantage of her generosity, and despised her kindness. She was truly showing me the love of God, and I kicked her in the teeth. Nancy Sullivan loved me anyway.

" But I'm a different person now. A new person. I sincerely apologize for my actions and attitude. I have asked God to forgive me. I hope you all will too."

She stopped and leaned back against the tree, and in just a few seconds, several women had their arms around her.

Sam stood up. "Libby, thank you for your courage and honesty. On behalf of Nancy Sullivan, I forgive you. I'm positive she would do so, if she were here. We all have been forgiven so much by God, that the least we can do is forgive each other. Welcome, Libby, and I hope you've been here long enough to get something to eat. There's plenty of food left if you haven't.

"And that reminds me. As I looked over the serving table full of the food you all have brought today, I began to see some familiar plates and bowls. They match a lot of the odd pieces of dinnerware in Bama's cupboard. I think many of you had been feeding her for quite a while. I went in and got the box I had put them in. They're up here on the porch. If you see anything you recognize, please take it home with you. Otherwise, you can buy it back at the auction."

People chuckled at that last remark, and it put Sam more at ease.

"I thank you all for being here, and providing this meal. And I especially want to thank Diana and Ted, Cherie and Nelson, for putting this special day together. I didn't have to do a thing."

Sam paused, took a deep breath and held up the poster in a plastic frame. It was her photo of the top of the pond lily desk. The caption read, "Look beyond the obvious. There's always something more. - Nancy Sullivan."

"I had this made for myself and my students, but I have one for you, too." She handed it over to Pastor Hitchcock. "If you want, you can hang it in the fellowship room, or youth room, or wherever."

"It's something Bama said to me a lot. It helped me become an artist, and it especially helped me see beyond the prickly teenage behavior of my students and become a better teacher. And when I allowed myself to look beyond my mother's dysfunctions, I could love the fearful, lonely woman underneath.

"But Bama didn't only say this, she lived it. She looked beyond this pale, abandoned infant and saw potential in me that she nurtured consistently. She looked beyond garlic as a crop or a hobby, and saw an opportunity to bless others. I know she gave away as much as she sold. And, as we've heard today, she looked beyond Libby's circumstances and attitudes and saw the grateful, godly woman she would become. Thanks again, Libby, for sharing your story with us.

"Well, as you might expect, I'm putting the house up for sale. I have a life back in California that is calling me. I really struggled with letting go of this place, but I've finally made peace with the fact that life is made up of change. You can't hold on to everything, no matter how much you might want to. So, I'm taking home a few mementoes, lots of photos, and some fond memories of this day that you all have given me. Thank you.

"And speaking of mementoes, there are hundreds of canning jars over here on the side porch. Please take them, if you can use them. And on this front table is a little gift of garlic for each of you. If you'd like to plant it, separate the cloves, but don't peel them. Put them in the ground in Sept. or October with the point up, just under the surface, and then bed them down for the winter with straw. That way, the part of Nancy Sullivan that was Royalty Garlic will live on in your own backyard. If you need more information about growing garlic, ask Google or Anna. Between them, they know everything there is."

Samantha paused and then said, "One last thing. If you've ever been here for coffee with Nancy, you'll recognize this." Sam held up the elderly French press. "You'll also remember that she always wrapped a dish towel around it, because the thing leaked. I'm sure several of you have had coffee dripped on your lap." A few chuckles and whispers throughout the crowd confirmed that suspicion.

"She refused to buy a Mr. Coffee, or a Keurig, because she didn't "want to get sucked in" to whatever the rest of the world was into. Well, she held out till the end." Sam lifted the coffee press up to the sky. "Good for you, Bama!" Then she hugged it to her chest for a minute.

Addressing the crowd, she said, "The funeral home had been holding her ashes for me. I picked them up earlier this week and sprinkled some on Grampy's grave. I have a little container to take back and bury next to her daughter."

She fingered the heart necklace she was wearing, "And there are some in this little locket. I'll wear it for a while. But at some point, I guess I'll drape it over the frame of her picture hanging on the wall at home.

"The remainder of her ashes are in this coffee pot. The funeral director assured me that the ashes are sterile, and Maine has no laws concerning what you can do with a person's remains. If you'd come with me, I'd like to bury this in the perennial bed out back. This coffee pot has been begging to be buried for decades.

"No need to let the new owners know what we've done. The flowers will close in over the spot, and no one needs to visit the place, because Bama is in heaven with Jesus...not here."

What Sam did not say was that also inside that coffee press was the little brass heart with her mother's ashes, that she'd found on Bama's bedside table. That gesture seemed to settle something in Samantha's soul. She didn't know why, exactly; her feelings about her mother were always so conflicted. But this felt right and proper.

Sam led the way around the house to the round flower bed that held the daylilies. Bright orange tiger lilies dominated the show, but Bama had planted probably 15 varieties over the years. Sam stepped up over the low rock border, and everyone else gathered around the circle. She looked at Pastor Hitchcock. "Sorry to spring this on you at the last minute, Pastor, but would you please?"

"Certainly." He stepped up and stood among the lilies.

"Friends, we have gathered today to celebrate the life of Nancy Noreen Sullivan. She was someone who truly knew how to love others. And now, we commit her ashes into the ground where they will be surrounded by the flowers that she planted and cared for. Father God, we know that you have already welcomed Nancy into your presence. By our actions today, we help Samantha put to rest the turmoil that a death creates. Give Sam the peace and the surety of your presence. We ask this in the name of the Father, Son and Holy Spirit. Amen." The circle of friends around them chorused, "Amen."

Samantha lowered the old coffee pot into the hole in the ground that Nelson had dug earlier. Then she picked a daylily blossom and tossed it in. "Please," she said to everyone else. "Feel free to pick the lilies. Take them home, or toss them in with the ashes. They'll be gone in the morning, anyway. They are a fitting symbol of the brevity and the beauty of our lives.

"Then let's go put some music on and see if there's any dessert left."

On the way past Nelson, she whispered, "Would you please close up the hole after everyone is done?"

He nodded and squeezed her arm.

Later, Cherie took Anna home. Nelson and Ted had taken off somewhere. When the last guest left, Samantha and Diana looked around the yard at the rumpled remains of a good party. Diana gave her a hug. "Go in and go to bed, Sam. We can clean this up tomorrow."

SAM WOKE up with the sun in her eyes. She looked out over the front lawn where a few hours before, almost fifty people had been milling about. There was not a trace of anything!

It was as though no one had been there. Not even a scrap of paper. And quite a few of the canning jars were gone, as well as the oddball dishes she had found in the cupboard.

All that was left was to shower, finish loading her car, and grab breakfast and coffee at the Blue Moose Café. The Adirondack chairs had been taken apart earlier in the week, and now lay flat and securely fastened to the roof rack, thanks to Ted. On the floor of the back seat was the coin collection, and the box with the *200 Jams and Preserves* cookbook and *Sister Wendy's Story of Painting*, as well as some jars of Bama-made pickle relish. She had added to that box, the little sign that said, "Wicked chickens lay deviled eggs." That would be a cute little piece of Maine to have in California.

Sam had also very carefully wrapped the little chicken crock that had held garlic on the kitchen counter. She had a narrow plastic tote that contained the quilt she and Bama had made and a piece she'd cut out of Bama's ancient bathrobe. Maybe she'd make a sofa pillow out of that, or something. She'd included the tote with her old sketchbooks, the zipped plastic bag that held the hardware from the chairs, and the "dictionary" safe with Bama's jewelry inside. On the back seat, she put her suitcase next to the box of garlic she was taking to use in her art classes, and to give to Marshall and Mrs. Springer.

At the last minute, she threw in a battered watering can, and several of the little turtles and frogs Bama had scattered to adorn the flower gardens.

Suddenly she panicked. Where was he? There was one frog that had to come home with her. His long legs were dangling out of Hawaiian print Bermuda shorts; he was relaxing in a frog-sized Adirondack chair, ice tea in his hand, sunglasses propped on his head. Bama had named him "Orkin" and said, "He's in charge of pest control. He doesn't have a very good work ethic, which is why there are so many bugs around here."

Sam ran around the flower gardens, lifting low-hanging branches and peering under bushes. She finally gave up, thinking he must surely have disappeared in the ensuing years.

She headed back to the car. As she went around the front to the driver's side, she dropped her keys. When she bent over to pick them up, a flash of white caught her eye.

The Black-eyed Susans stood there, laughing at her in the breeze. Tucked beneath them was the guy she had been looking for. Nearly all of his color had faded away, and the leg of his chair was broken off. She had practically stepped on him a hundred times while she was here, and never noticed him until now. She wrapped him in a bunch of paper towels and added him to her load.

The irony that this silly frog represented was not lost on her. She had another guy that she'd been stepping around for years and never noticed. But she'd see him in a week or so, and be sure to change that.

At last, Samantha forced herself to take a few deep breaths and drive down the driveway; it made it a little easier to pretend she was only going for breakfast.

After a quick stop, Sam headed south on Route 1, and when she came to the turnout overlooking the ocean, she pulled over and got out of the car for another breath of clean Maine air. The salty seaweed fragrance refreshed her and gave her both a stab of pain in her heart and a new burst of energy.

She stood and looked out over the guardrail at the ocean. It certainly felt different than the night she had first driven up here. She was struck with the thought that this was a picture of her life. Underneath all the clouds and fog of her childhood was a beautiful green coastline, amazing boulders, a powerful ocean, and a brilliant blue sky.

"Well, that's it. Thanks, Lord. Couldna' done it without you. Please keep me safe on the trip home."

She sent off a text to Marshall. *Headed south, then west. See you in about a week.*

EPILOGUE

Thirteen years later

The Jeep pulled off the road in front of the farmstand, but Anna didn't get out right away.

"Well, Ginger, we did it. All over now but the ceremony. Thanks for being my transportation. The DMV is really picky about who they let behind the wheel. You've been a life-saver these last few months."

"No problem, Anna. Glad to do it."

Anna asked, "I guess next semester, you're headed up to Fort Kent for more nursing school, right?"

"Yep." said Ginger. "How about you? Are you going for your Bachelor's?"

Anna shook her head. "No, I don't want to study business anymore; I want to DO business. In fact, if you have a few minutes, come with me, up the hill behind the house. I want to show you the pole barn my dad and I are building."

They walked around to the back of the house and up

through the path cutting through the woods. In the field stood the skeleton of a large barn.

Anna held the front door to usher in her guest, even though there was a huge opening a few inches away where a garage door would be installed.

"You'll have to use your imagination inside here. To your right we have a staircase that leads to the loft where I'll dry the garlic. Just beyond that is my office. Then in the back on the right is the kitchen.

"Opposite the kitchen is the packing and shipping area which conveniently connects to the overhead door up front here to accommodate a delivery van."

Ginger wandered back to the unfinished kitchen area and ran her hand over a large stainless-steel box sitting on the floor. "What's this? A dishwasher?"

"No," said Anna. "That is every last penny of last year's garlic profit. It's a dehydrator so I can get our 'Thyme In a Bottle' business up and running, even when the weather is too damp for herbs to dry upstairs."

The plan was for the whole loft to be racks of screens. Both ends would open up for maximum airflow, but the windows were set far back under the overhang so rain would not be an issue.

"This is so cool, Anna. I knew about the farmstand and the garlic, but I can see now, when things get going here, you won't have time for more school. Good on you!"

"Thanks! We should have the building done by fall, I think. Hopefully the loft will be finished this summer in time for the garlic harvest. Dad's anxious to have his garage back."

Anna walked Ginger back to her car. "See you Saturday for pomp and circumstance!"

After her friend pulled out, she went into the garage and sat down at her little desk.

She got out a sheet of paper, and her sharpie.

In large black letters she wrote:

Hey guys! Hope you are all well. The bulbs I'm sending are small and may be a little too dry; it's pretty much the end of the line.

Speaking of the end, I'm done with school! Last final today. Ceremony Saturday. Woohoo!!

Mom and Dad send their love. Hug the munchkins for me, and tell them I need more art for my refrigerator. I'll do a complete building project update at our regular Facetime next month.

Love, Anna

She carefully placed 4 garlics in a little box with her note, sealed it and added the gold starburst label to the upper left corner. The chubby, crown-wearing garlic bulb smiled back at her. Royalty Garlic was alive and well.

In the address area she wrote:

Marshall and Samantha Mayfield
193 Roosevelt Ave
North Hills, CA 91343

AUTHOR'S NOTE

Dear Reader,

If you've been thinking that "Royalty" is an odd name for a town, check out the list below. They're all names of real towns in Maine.

Temple
Freedom
Liberty
Strong
Friendship
Industry

Go figure!

Wendy